My Elvis Blackout

My Elvis Blackout

Simon Crump

BLOOMSBURY

First published in Great Britain 2000
This paperback edition published 2001

Copyright © 2000 by Simon Crump

The moral right of the author has been asserted

Bloomsbury Publishing Plc, 38 Soho Square, London W1D 3HB

A CIP catalogue record for this book
is available from the British Library

ISBN 0 7475 5376 9

10 9 8 7 6 5 4 3 2 1

Typeset by Hewer Text Ltd, Edinburgh
Printed in Great Britain by Clays Ltd, St Ives plc

for Duncan McLean
Compañero!

Contents

1   Valleyville   1
2   International Hotel   3
3   Scatter   5
4   High School Story:
    Angie Crumbaker c. 1959   9
5   Fun, Fun, Fun   17
6   Lady in Red   23
7   Elvis: Fat Fucked-up Fool   29
8   Ex-Elvis   31
9   Elvis: Fat Fucked-up Foetus   33
10 Gladys   35
11 August 1970   37
12 Gladys: Part Two   41
13 Perfect Crime   45
14 Elvis and His Mom Were Lovers   49
15 Diary of Larry Geller, Elvis's
    Hairdresser and Spiritual Guide   51
16 An Amazing Talk with Elvis   55

17 An Amazing Talk with Elvis: Part Two   *57*

18 An Amazing Talk with Elvis: Part Three   *61*

19 An Amazing Talk with Elvis: Part Four   *65*

20 Stairway to Heaven   *69*

21 Jungle Room   *75*

22 Lansky Brothers   *79*

23 From Elvis's Secret Diary   *87*

24 From Elvis's Secret Diary: Part Two   *89*

25 Fame & Fortune   *93*

26 Country Song   *95*

27 Downtown   *99*

28 Noline   *103*

29 Elvis Cookbook   *109*

30 Twinkletown   *113*

31 Loma Linda   *121*

32 Yorkshire Elvis   *127*

33 Yorkshire Elvis: Part Two   *129*

34 My Elvis Blackout   *135*

35 From Elvis's Secret Diary: Part Three   *137*

36 From Elvis's Secret Diary: Part Four   *139*

37 Elvis's Spotter's Guide   *143*

Acknowledgements   *145*

Valleyville

Consider this. When I met Elvis outside the Wig Market, I was the typical housewife: two children – Teddy and Jody, both boys – and a house that would be paid up by the time we reached our fifties. Elvis was very active in our church, and he was forever attending meetings. I suppose his job – he was head of the glassware department in one of our bigger stores – didn't demand too much of him, and besides, Elvis liked doing things for people.

Elvis came by for me Saturday night in a battered old pickup truck. 'Hope you don't mind the heap,' he said. 'I had a sports car, but I had to sell it. I'm going to get another – a red one with black leather upholstery.' I knew that he was lying, he'd been driving that old pickup for years.

'Where shall we go, doll?' he asked grandly, as if we were in Paris with a dozen glamorous nightclubs to choose from. Actually, Valleyville had only one night-club, a dark little hole down by the tracks. No nice girl went there.

We drove to Crown Point. It was quiet there and beautiful. We bumped into Barbara Cartland. 'The little town lay below us like a splash of stars fallen from the Milky Way. All about us was the dark forest of pines and the wide, clear sky that seemed to stretch for ever,' she said. We buried her mutilated body in the woods.

Elvis took a hose from the back of the pickup, fixed it to the exhaust and ran it through the window. He started the engine. We'd been dead for hours when the cops found us.

International Hotel

I know the chicks at home gonna jump and shout when they hear old Charlie Manson busted out, he's a kiiiller and he's gonna stop by your house, he got Sharon Tate and it's too late, you better lock your gate and stay quiet as a little fucking mouse . . .

'Turn that shit off now!' barks Elvis. 'I hate those fuckin' Osmonds, they're a whole bunch of faggots and Jews, an' I hate Jews, an' faggot Jews! I'd like to blow all those bastards away!'

'Yeah, sure thing, boss, OK.' I reach for the radio, but before I get to the switch he whips out his .38 and blasts the fucking thing right out of the window. Fragments of Japanese Solid State shower the crowd gathered below outside the International Hotel. Most of them have been waiting all day, sweltering in the heat reflected off their own cars. Middle-aged women doused with hairspray, younger women playing hookey from their day-jobs, kids who should be in school, even a hippie pulling on a joint.

Elvis folds back a corner of the foil pasted to the window. 'Jesus, Larry, I love those people, all except that fuckin' hippie, I wouldn't be here without those other damn female guys. See how that Coke bottle sits merrily atop yonder Del Fuego Automobile?'

'Boss?'

He pulls out the .38 again and starts blasting away, the crowd scatters. Each time he misses the Coke by a country mile. 'Sheeet!' he screams, and dashes into another room. Ten seconds later he's back, he's naked now and carrying a 30.06 deer-hunting rifle. 'AHA-HAHAHAHA! this motherfucker should get the job done,' he laughs, and takes aim at the Coke. Just then I notice that he's got 'Live at the International Hotel, Vegas' scrawled on the end of his dick in Biro. The rifle's got a telescopic sight and's accurate up to a quarter of a mile, so I figure even that asshole Elvis can hit the damn bottle now.

Scatter

A few months before Elvis joined the army his entourage took on a new member, a forty-pound chimpanzee called Scatter. His trainer, Bill Killebrew, used both Scatter and his younger brother, Chatter, on a Memphis children's TV show. Elvis and the guys weren't exactly cruel to the chimp, but they did give him a pretty hard time.

Daytimes, Scatter was a total pain in the butt. He'd masturbate in public, he'd shit in his hands and throw it on the walls. He drank bourbon, he bit the staff at Graceland, and whenever he got the chance he put his dick in people's drinks.

Nights, Scatter sat alone in his cage, rocking back and forth, crying to himself. He loved his kid brother and missed him terribly. He longed to be with Chatter again, and all the while he was trying to figure out a way to rescue him from the humiliation of his life in TV land.

As soon as Elvis was processed out of the army he returned to Graceland. The house was in an awful state. The roof had leaked destroying a great deal of the interior decor and all the roses in the Meditation Garden had died. His pets had starved to death. It was a pitiful sight. Out in the yard, Elvis's pet turkey, Bow-Tie, was a heap of bone and rotting feathers and the three donkeys which Elvis had been keeping in the empty swimming pool while the perimeter fence was being built were now just bleached skeletons, even Rising Sun, his prize stallion, was frozen dead in his stall.

Scatter was alive and well. He was bigger, louder and even hairier than before. He was wearing a bell-hop's uniform. He'd bitten off the trousers and jacket to something approaching the right lengths and he looked a lot like Robinson Crusoe, only in the chimp re-make. When he saw Elvis he whooped with joy, came lolloping towards him on all fours, and extended his right hand which Elvis shook warmly. Scatter had shat in his hands about a minute before.

Since the death of his wife, Vernon, Elvis's daddy, had become a hopeless drunk and made no attempt to run the house while Elvis was away, so as he pushed open the front door Elvis was confronted by mountains of unopened mail. He felt better then, because he thought it was fanmail, but in fact it was nearly all bills.

He called up Roy Orbison, who he'd recorded with in the early days when they were both still signed to Sam Phillips's Sun label.

Roy was down on his luck as well. He'd been showing off in front of his few remaining fans. He'd written his name in lighter fluid on a glass-topped coffee table, set it afire and burned his house down. His second wife, Claudette, had run off with one of the firemen, and his daughter who was passing by on her motorcycle had been so distracted by the blaze that she'd ridden straight into a tree and broken her back in three places. His dog had just died and ten minutes before Elvis called him up, Roy had found out that he only had six months to live, plus he'd worn dark glasses for so long that the skin on the bridge of his nose had grown around them so he couldn't take them off now, even if he wanted to. On top of all that he was flat broke.

Between them they decided to hit a bank in Mart, a little town eighteen miles south-east of Waco. They set off in Elvis's blue '54 Fleetwood limousine. About halfway into the trip they pulled up at a roadside diner. Alongside the usual motley collection of beat-up Fords and Chevys parked out front, Elvis spotted a shiny new Messerschmitt three-wheeler micro-car, just like the one he'd bought while he was on National Service in Germany. As the limo swung on to the gravel of the front lot, the little car fired up and sped off along the interstate.

Elvis and Roy arrived in Mart. They robbed the bank. Everything went exactly according to plan. It was so easy that it was almost a disappointment. They never got to shoot or hit or even shout at anybody, and it was all over in a matter of minutes.

Back outside on the pavement, Roy stopped to sign some autographs for a few fans who hadn't perished in the fire and just for a moment Elvis put the bag which contained the loot on the hood of the Fleetwood while he fumbled for his keys.

Elvis heard the throb of the Messerschmitt's two-stroke engine, saw a hairy hand reach out and seize the bag and seconds later the three-wheeler was a dot on the horizon.

Scatter steered the Messerschmitt into a side street and switched off the motor. He turned to his brother. They hugged each other for a long time and then shouted with delight.

'I told you it would work,' Scatter said, and their tiny car roared off, way down the yellow-brick road.

Into a perfect sunset.

High School Story:
Angie Crumbaker *c.* 1959

Mom had just finished helping me slip into my frothy
new formal when the telephone rang. 'It's probably
your father,' she said as she regarded me critically. I
told him to close the drugstore early today so he could
see how lovely you look for the prom.' 'Well he'd
better get here right away!' I told her. 'Elvis said he'd
pick me up at eight sharp.'

I twirled in front of the full-length mirror, my heart
beating with excitement. I did look lovely! So lovely I
was sure Elvis would catch me close and say, 'Oh
Angie, I love you so much!'

And I loved Elvis Presley with all my heart and soul.
I could just think of his blue eyes and his sculpted
sandy hair and get weak-kneed. He was sweet and
steady and tender too. Why couldn't my mother see
those qualities also? Why did she have to judge because his mother had a bunch of ragamuffin kids and
was remarried to that old stepfather of Elvis's who
kept her pregnant all the time?

Any other woman would have walked out on some-one like Jud Cusick, but Elvis's mother belonged to a strict religion, the World-Wide Beholders. The women had to wear long green skirts and yellow bonnets, and were, as Elvis had tried to explain, beholden to their husbands' every wish and command.

'Mom must have rebelled from the religion just once,' he told me, 'when she ran away with my dad. He wasn't one of them, and for a while they were real happy. Then Dad was killed in a mine cave-in, and because I was just a baby, Mom was forced to return to her religious settlement.'

Mom was calling me to the phone. 'It's Elvis,' she said. 'He sounds odd, like he's been drinking.' Her mouth tightened as she handed me the receiver. 'Oh honey! I wish you were going to the dance with Clark Wothington or that nice Harold Amory.'

'Oh please, Mom!' I begged, my hand hard against the receiver so Elvis wouldn't hear. She clucked her tongue and walked away, and I said, 'Elvis? What's wrong?'

He did sound funny, almost like he was crying. 'Could you come down here right away? Please, Angie I need you, oh Angie I need you so much, honey!'

'I'll be right there,' I promised. 'Dad's due home, and he'll drive me.' Then lower so Mom couldn't hear, I said, 'And I love you, Elvis!'

Mom had ten cat fits when I started getting out of the new formal she'd slaved over for weeks and into the first skirt and sweater I could grab from the closet. She begged me to call around and see if there was some other boy in the seniors who didn't have a date and who could take me. I just kept telling her that I had to be with Elvis. Besides, I never could have danced and had fun, knowing he was alone and miserable.

My formal hung in the closet like a limp neglected flower. I wondered if I'd ever be able to wear it as Elvis's girl. I thought of the times Elvis and I had let our kisses get too long and wild. My skin felt warm as I remembered.

Dad was pretty grim about the whole deal too, but he agreed to drive me and made me promise to call him up the minute I needed a ride home.

My chin quivered as we approached the house. 'Oh Daddy! When Elvis suffers, I just suffer too. I can't help it.' I wiped my eyes and nose, then tried to smile. 'And as far as the prom goes, it really doesn't matter.'

It did though, and I knew I had just been crying for that, too. I had missed a lot of fun this year by being Elvis's girl. Yet I didn't blame him. It certainly wasn't his fault that he had problems. But sometimes I wished he had an entirely different family from that offbeat strange outfit he came from!

Elvis was in his room, his head buried in his hands. His blue eyes were filled with bleakness as he looked up at me. 'Angie, I have something to tell you, I've killed someone!' he said miserably. My head swam, I could feel blood pumping in my ears, sickness chugged into my throat. 'Oh Elvis,' I said. 'What . . . where . . . how . . . who . . .?' I felt my voice trail off.

'This afternoon,' he moaned. 'I was driving Pa's sedan up by Strawberry Point, I saw Sylvie Carlin hitching a ride, her old jalopy had a flat and she needed a ride back into town. I picked her up, and suggested she come back to our place to use the phone. Pa had gone over to Moses Keefe's house to have a tooth pulled, and Ma was at Bible class and . . . I . . . Oh honey . . .' Suddenly he crushed me to him, his lips covering mine, and I started to sob.

'Elvis, please tell me what's going on!' I begged. 'I can't stand it, I love you too much!'

'Shh hon,' he crooned, calmer now. 'It's all right, Angie, stop crying.' He straightened me up, brushing away my tears. 'I didn't want to tell you, but now I guess I have to.'

He looked so grim I lost my breath.

'For the last couple of months . . . well . . . I've been stealing wigs from Eveline's House of Hair and Feminine Beauty, taking them back home and shampooing them, I just can't stop myself, it makes me feel so good. So I asked maybe I could wash her hair?'

'Oh my God,' I whimpered. I pulled away from Elvis, my head spinning with the horrible things he was telling me.

Elvis's dark brows drew together in a frown. I could feel his fingers gripping my arm. If I live to be a thousand I'll never forget the way his face looked. His voice sounded thick and slurred. 'So, I washed her hair, and, boy, it felt so good I did it again, she got kinda scared and I had to tie her to the chair.'

I had to clamp down hard on my teeth to keep them from chattering. I felt hurt and sick inside, unable to bear the vivid sight of Sylvia and Elvis together, the sight that ripped across my mind like a colourful nightmare. I began to cry again.

'All right!' he cried. 'So what! Stop acting like a nitwit, Angie, what harm's done?' He banged a fist against his bedroom wall. 'No one's been hurt!'

My voice rose to a hysterical pitch, I was really crying now. It was so shocking, so horrible! 'No harm done! No harm! Just now you said you'd killed someone today, was it Sylvie? Well was it?'

'Oh yeah,' he said, quite calmly now. 'I forgot, I must've tied her a bit too tight, coz I went out for more shampoo, and when I came back she was blue and her tongue was sticking out of her mouth. She's in the closet now.'

There was a lump in my throat so big I couldn't swallow. I kept choking on it. Yet I'd always been jealous of Sylvie with her flame-red hair, her shapely legs and flashy clothes, and the more I thought about her prancing around in her tight dress with all the boys chasing after her the more I was glad that she was dead.

After a long moment, Elvis slipped an arm around my shoulders. 'Sometimes we do silly things that we regret later, honey,' he whispered. Then he flashed me a wide smile, a smile so young and carefree I felt I must have imagined the cloud that hung over him a few moments before.

I snuggled over close, tucking my hand through his arm. 'You could wear your hair in pigtails and go around in overalls, and I'd still love you,' I smiled.

'Uh, hold on a minute then there, hon,' Elvis drawled, and he disappeared into the kitchen. When he came back out a few minutes later he had on a long auburn wig tied into two thick bunches with scarlet ribbons and a navy cotton overall which had the words Crown Electric Co. embroidered across the chest by his aged alcoholic mother. He'd hastily applied some lipstick and he'd printed 'I AM NOT

WEARING A WIG' across his forehead in Maybelline Ultra*Shadow Heavenly Purple eyeliner.

At that moment Elvis looked so handsome that my aching heart began to bleed.

Fun, Fun, Fun

I met Elvis through my brother, Red, who'd been with him since high school. He was very close to Elvis, and over the years I got to know him pretty well too, until eventually I became one of the team, the Memphis Mafia, as we liked to call ourselves.

On this particular night, Elvis held open house. His place in Bel Air was made for fun and games. Apart from its lavish furnishings, there was a special party room which contained every conceivable kind of pinball game. In the centre of the room was a large competition-size pool table. The room was on a lower level. Steps from the games room took you into a gigantic living room. I knew that there were going to be a few of the guys around having a party.

The final filming for *Fun in Acapulco* was over and everybody was winding down. I was at International House of Pancakes down on the Strip, and picked up on these two pretty girls. One of the girls later became quite a well-known actress, but it was the other one (let's call her Judy), who I was interested in.

Anyway, I took them up to the house and there is a whole thing going on up there. Depending on what sort of mood he is in, Elvis on one of these nights just might say hullo to everybody and go straight to bed. Other nights he wouldn't even come down at all, but if he was looking around for a little action, he would sweet-talk some gal for a while and then take her upstairs. On this night, Elvis didn't seem to be doing any of these things. He was all dressed up and carrying one of his canes; he'd had a whole bunch of them custom-made after he saw *Dr Jekyll and Mr Hyde* at the movies. In fact they were sword canes with a dagger in the bottom, just like the one Mr Hyde carries in the picture. Elvis was looking pretty tired and seemed a bit agitated. I walked in and gave him a big hullo. He wanted me to play pool with him. Now I had these ladies with me, but when Elvis wants you to do something, you do it. So I left these two little gals to all the other vultures up there and started to play pool with Elvis.

After a while we started playing four-handed pool with two other guys at the party. Elvis's mood was not being helped any by the fact that he was muffing about every second shot. I was getting tense, knowing that E's temper can flash in these situations. What made me more worried was the fact that there were a lot of people around, lots of chicks, and I was scared that he would do something in front of them all. It was only a couple of months since I'd buried a guy that Elvis had wasted, he'd cut this dude's head off while he was asleep, saying he sure thought it would be funny to see what he said when he woke up and found that his head was missing. Well . . . we all laughed at the time, but it was me who had to dispose of the poor guy's body when he didn't wake up.

Anyway, by this time Judy had gotten bored with the party, she came over and said to me, 'I think I'd better be leaving now. Could you move your car please? It's blocking mine and I can't get out.'

Elvis rose slowly from the table where he was about to hit a shot. 'What in the hell does she want?'

'Nothing, boss. She just wants me to move my car so she can get out.'

That didn't satisfy Elvis. 'Whoa there . . . Hell, man, you're playing pool. Let her get someone else to move the damn car.'

Judy flushed with embarrassment. She had never met Elvis before and now here she was falling out with him. Judy replied, 'Look, I sure am sorry, I just don't know anyone else here to ask. That's why I asked him. And' – looking at me – 'mister, if you just move it, I'll leave. I'm sorry to bother you.' Judy looked like she wanted to jump into a hole someplace. Elvis Presley's

19

eyes narrowed, he pulled himself upright and his lips curled back. I knew the signs.

Elvis grabs his damn cane and jumps up on to the pool table, his eyes bugging out of his head and the sweat oozing down his face. He starts giving us the goddamn Sermon on the Mount. But the way he gave it was a little different from the Bible. He stood there, held up his hands for silence, and in a loud preacher's voice he yelled down to us as we stood around with our faces turned up to him, 'Whoa, all ye motherfuckers, of kind thoughts and good deeds . . .'

The stupid cocksucker went on in this vein on for some time and it really was funny. There was a bunch of girls there sitting on the floor, and when they saw that we weren't laughing, because we knew better, they kept their faces straight like they were in church listening to a sermon. Anyway, he starts talking about Moses, and he says, his voice still like some crazy bastard gospel preacher, 'Moses, that white-haired sonofabitch, comes running down from this big mountain. Now his damn hair has turned white because he has seen the Lord, and those things happen when you see the Lord. Anyway, he came on down from the mountain, and how he got down was the burning bushes directed his ass on down.'

Then he starts talking about Jesus. 'Now Jesus,' he says, 'is getting it on with Mary Magdalene, you know, the woman at the well. It ain't in the Bible but it's true. She got stoned, but Jesus took care of her and they travelled around a lot together.'

I look over at Red, my brother, and he's biting his sleeve trying not to laugh, looking like he might have a heart attack any minute. Several of the other guys have tears running down their faces, but nobody dares laugh, as there's no telling what Elvis might do.

'Alleluia,' he says.

'Alleluia,' we all say.

Suddenly Elvis's face comes over more peaceful. Then he says, 'Jesus said he was old and of age and *** ll ass backwards in the dust.' By this time I want to la** *** so bad I think I'm gonna puke.

'Amen,' says the fat fucker.

'Amen,' we all say.

Just as I'm thinking, that's it . . . thank fuck for that, he's through, and looking for my car keys so I can let poor Judy out of this nut-house, Elvis looks straight into the poor kid's eyes and in a soft voice he says, 'Come here my child, approach the sacred altar.'

So Judy walks up to the pool table, all the while smiling nervously at Elvis.

'Shut your eyes and open your mouth, and see what the King would give you,' he murmurs in that same gentle voice.

Oh shit, I'm thinking, he's gonna whip out Little

Pink Elvis and shove it in Judy's mush – I can just picture that splashed across the front of the *Hicksville Exaggerator*.

Anyway, Judy does as he asks, and before any of us know what's happening Elvis pulls out his swordstick and slashes her right across the windpipe. She's lying on the carpet, blood pumping out her throat, and everybody's yelling at Elvis and screaming for an ambulance.

'Hell,' Elvis says. 'It ain't nothin', she's alright. It was just one of those dramatic falls. Drag her ass out of here.'

I grab Judy's ankles and haul her into the corridor. After that I fetch my shovel from the garage.

Lady in Red

Elvis came out of the trailer which served as his dressing room on the set of the movie *Live a Little, Love a Little (Drink a Lot)*.

Chris de Burgh was waiting to see him, he'd been hanging around for ages, trying to get an autograph, and he was so happy to finally meet Elvis that the sad little man broke into song . . .

'A spaceman came travelling, in his ship from afar – twas light years of time since his mission did start, and over a village he halted his craft and it hung in the sky like a star, just like a star.'

'That really was very poor,' Elvis said calmly.

'AM I SUPPOSED TO BE IMPRESSED BY THAT SHIT?' he screamed, then turned to me . . .

'Execute this reedy-voiced, ferret-faced little bastard NOW!'

It was pretty soon after the time when Elvis had been abducted by aliens and he was still very touchy about the whole topic of intergalactic space travel. He'd just been to see the film *Chariots of Fire*. He thought it was an Erich von Däniken picture. One of Elvis's favourite books was von Däniken's *Chariots of the Gods?* and he'd hoped that the film version would help him come to terms with his own experience.

When he'd realised that it was about a bunch of faggoty English guys running around on a beach he went completely berserk and burned out the theatre. Which reminds me, when I catch up with him, that Colin Welland dude is sure gonna be sorry.

Anyway, so I twisted Chris's weedy arm up behind his back and marched him round the side of the trailer. I jammed the muzzle of my .38 in his mush and blammo! that little fucker wouldn't be dancing with the Lady in Red any more.

That evening, after the day's filming had ended, me and a few of the guys were sitting around with Elvis in his trailer, drinking tequila slammers and playing blackjack.

I heard this scratching sound coming from outside like there was a cat or a wild animal or something trying to get in. I opened the door a couple of inches and damn me if it wasn't Chris de Burgh back from the fucking dead.

His head was completely gone, there was just a bloodied stump sticking out of his satin bomber jacket, but in a way he kinda looked a lot better, more human almost.

'Hey guys!' I yelled. 'It's Chris de Burgh, back from the fucking dead!'

Anyway, I helped him up the little metal steps into the trailer. So, he's just stood there silhouetted in the doorway and we're all gawking at the empty space above his shoulders where by rights a head ought to be.

Suddenly this low booming voice like a 45 on 33 starts coming out of Chris's chest.

'Hey fellas, there's something I have to tell you, can I take a moment of your time?'

'Yeah, sure thing, Chris baby,' we all say in chorus, like some dumb Sunday Bible class. 'If you got something you need to share with us, then you go right on ahead.'

Frankly, I was a little worried. I'd wasted plenty of guys before, well obviously, it's kinda like a hobby to me, but Chris was definitely the first one who'd stopped by for a chat afterwards.

What if he wouldn't leave? It wasn't like I could blow his head off again or anything. Then I figured, 'I know, if he gets rude or nasty or bleeds on the rug or makes Elvis mad, I'll blow his legs off and shove his body in the trash,' so after that I felt a bit easier.

I got him settled nice and cosy in one of the folding canvas chairs which Elvis had ordered for all the Memphis Mafia when we got started in the movie business. I put a baseball cap over the stump coz close-up it was kinda unsightly and fixed the guy a drink.

So, he starts telling us what it is he needs to say. His diction seemed a little strange to me, but then I remember that the guy's English so that's probably why he sounds like such a fucking pansy.

'After eight years of pains I received the stigmata at the age of thirty-one on the twentieth of September 1973; my wounds opened up and released a great deal of blood. For me as for many stigmatics, my marks were very painful.

'I had a vision, just about the time I recorded that great song "Don't Pay the Ferryman"' . . . and his voice trails off like he's remembering the song.

At this point I can see that the other guys are thinking about that song too, they're getting angry and Elvis's face has gone a funny purple colour.

'Yeah anyway, Chris. Forget that dumb song, tell us about the vision,' I say.

'I saw before me a mysterious person . . . his hands and feet and side were dripping with blood. The vision disappeared and I became aware that my hands, feet and side were dripping blood. Imagine the agony I experienced and continue to experience almost every day. I am dying of pain from the wounds and because I like to wear white clothes and move about a lot on stage, I suffer from perpetual seepage-based, stain-oriented embarrassment.'

'Well, thanks very much for telling us about that, Chris,' we all say in chorus again, then I take him outside and blow his legs off.

Elvis: Fat Fucked-up Fool

His greatest fear was of being poor and he dwelled upon it constantly. He took handfuls of jewels and cash into the backyard at Graceland and buried them – little treasures to call upon should he suddenly find himself penniless. The guys would watch Elvis digging in the dark. He cut a pathetic figure as he grunted and sweated over a growing heap of earth, and they would laugh to see his white jump-suit soiled with mud, and they would laugh at this very sad, but nevertheless highly entertaining creature trying to ward off his worst nightmare, and they would laugh and laugh and laugh until the tears ran down their bloated piggy faces and down their fat pink necks and into their fancy silk shirts which Elvis had bought them all from Lansky Brothers, because he loved them so.

They never tried to stop him; they knew how violent he could become if you got in his way, especially these days when he always carried a gun, and they also knew he was so drugged that, come sunup when he was still sleeping, they could dig the stuff up and divide it among themselves, secure in the knowledge that the fat fool would remember nothing of his handiwork by the time they roused him the following afternoon.

Some of the guys genuinely loved Elvis. Nearly all of them mimicked him in his habits, actions and dress, although not quite to the extent where they would fuck fourteen-year-old girls three at a time, eat five quarts of ice-cream at one sitting, claim to be Jesus H. Christ, wear incontinence pants under a purple cape and bury their valuables in the yard. However, they did really and truly respect him in the artistic sense, and as a human being, and it has to be said that he set a fine example for all Americans as to how they should live their lives come the happy day they became paranoid prescription drug addicts.

Ex-Elvis

Anyone who has walked across a carpet that is bellying up with the underfloor draught will know what I mean.

Way back home there's a funeral.

All the police carry guns.

Something she said worries him.

Somebody stole his crown.

Sometimes he cries in his sleep.

All he has is a radio and a guitar.

There's a pain in his chest and he throws up all the time.

His last album sold only five copies.

The long black dream is over.

Time to get some rest.

He retunes the radio to State Hospital FM.

He slumps down in his easy chair.

Then he dies.

Elvis: Fat Fucked-up Foetus

When he was a foetus, Elvis used to wait till his Mom was asleep, carefully remove his umbilical cord, sneak out of her insides and head off into town. He usually wore the little tartan coat which Alfredo, their disgusting toy poodle, wore for his walks with Momsy on cold winter mornings. Elvis looked like a complete tosser in this outfit, what with the blood and the dog hairs, but what the fuck did he care? He was the unborn King of Rock 'n' Roll and if he wanted to go out naked except for a ridiculous tartan dog coat, he bastard well would. He'd steal cans of Delmonte pineapple chunks from the Magic Market on Centenary Road, Goole, England.

'Now's the time to rip stuff off,' he figured.

'Before I get any goddamn fingerprints.'

One time when he got home he tried to crawl back inside Alfredo by mistake, but as any fool knows, you can't get to heaven in a biscuit tin (coz a biscuit tin's got biscuits in) and you can't fit an embryo up a dog's arse.

Gladys

Elvis was a long and difficult birth, boy, did he give me a hard time!

I was thirty-one hours in labour with him, pushing all that time. Today it would be a forceps or Caesarian birth, I suppose.

They told me, 'It's a little boy.' But he was the most horrible colour and his head was so misshapen that it was unbelievable. The reason for it being a difficult birth was that his arm had twisted up towards his head during delivery. You can see the scar on his head in his baby photographs; they told me that if it had been any closer to his left eye he could have lost the sight of it.

I asked if there were any other problems. I pointed out to nurse that he didn't seem to be breathing and asked what was the matter with him.

'He's dead,' she told me. 'Oh Gladys, I'm so sorry, but I thought that was obvious.'

He seemed quite normal to me, I breast-fed him, he laughed, he cried, he was a good baby, a quiet baby. But his head was a bit too big.

August 1970

We went into Kerr's Sporting Goods one time and Elvis saw a real pretty .22. It was engraved and he bought it. Then in '70, he went in there on a spree and bought thirty-two handguns, a shotgun and a rifle. That included a .44 Ruger Blackhawk gold-plated revolver which cost $1,850, and a .357 Colt Python revolver, which set him back $1,950. The total bill came to $19,792. Red's still got the receipt.

In the backyard at Graceland there's a big old lime tree and one late August afternoon in 1970, me, Elvis and my kid brother Red are using it for a spot of target practice. I'm using my navy issue Colt, Red's got a M101 Duramatic pistol and Elvis is using his fancy fucking lah-di-dah gold-plated Blackhawk.

We've got beercans, Coke bottles and some teddy bears that the fans are always sending in for Elvis all set up in the branches and we're blasting away like it's going out of fashion. We take it in turns to go up a ladder and prop the stuff back in the tree while the other two guys reload and then off we go again.

Gladys staggers out of the back kitchen door to see what's going on. As per usual for this time of day she's completely wasted on her favourite combo of diet pills and cheap wine. She asks Elvis if she can have a try, we all exchange *OhmyGod*-type glances but he says, 'Yeah, OK, sure thing, Mom, but you gotta set up the targets first.' So she totters across the lawn, slowly climbs the ladder and crouches in a fork in the branches where she starts setting up the cans and shit. Elvis puts fresh bullets into his pistol, turns to me and smiles. 'Now ain't that somethin',' he drawls, and for one awful moment I think maybe he's going to blow his mom away.

Just then there's this Godawful scream and Gladys comes crashing out of the tree, hits the deck with a thud, and starts thrashing around in the long grass at the edge of the lawn, all the while hollering like a stuck pig.

So we go charging across the lawn to where the drunken old bird is having her shit-fit and then we see that she's completely covered in ants, great big green motherfuckers. I reckon they must've smelled the alcohol on her while she was up in the tree and figured she was lunch. Come to think of it, Elvis claimed to have seen some huge ants a coupla days before, but we thought it was just the usual drugged-up crap he's always talking. Anyway, right after we all stop laughing, Elvis tears off his shirt and starts flapping it over his mom to scare the ants away, and me and Red make a run for the kitchen to fetch buckets of water.

When we get back she's quiet and Elvis is kneeling next to her.

'Too late, guys,' he says, 'she's gone.'

And boy was it too late, and Holy Shit was she gone. Them flippin' ants had eaten up just about every part of Gladys except her dentures, her jewellery and some of her hair.

Damnedest thing I ever saw.

Gladys: Part Two

At first I reckoned I'd been bitten by them flipping ants, I'd noticed them running around everywhere.

I lifted my blouse to see where the itch was coming from. It looked like a smile. There was a red mark on my side, like a U-shape, just under my ribs.

I held an orange in my hand, and then had this extraordinary spiritual feeling. A feeling of complete tranquillity engulfed me. My perspective completely shifted. I thought, I can face anything now, because of a feeling from holding this simple object, grown from the earth.

I looked down at my feet, there was very thick blood coming out of my shoes. I took them off but when I came to remove my socks they had stuck to the wounds and I had to tear them away.

They were full, raw crater-like things, open wounds weeping and bleeding. I put a square bit of non-stick plaster over them. Then I rang Doctor Nichopoulos and put the kettle on for a cup of tea.

I thought I'd better try the bomb out, so I connected up the batteries and switched on. There was a loud pop and acrid black smoke quickly filled the room. I disconnected it, opened all the windows and undid the screws on the front of the control panel.

The component which had failed, a capacitor between the input and the timer, was easy to spot as it was still on fire.

I snipped out what was left of it and headed off towards my local electrical spares shop carrying its charred little corpse in a matchbox. They have a sign over the counter which reads:

SHOPLIFTING MAKES
YER NOSE BLEED.

You get a lot of mentally retarded CB bores in there and the odd wild-eyed dandruff-covered type who's spent the last ten years desperately trying to build a robot that will have sex with him.

On my way there I saw an old blind lady with a dog in a harness walking uncertainly up the hill. On the way back, with my new capacitor lying in the box next to its dead relative, I saw the old lady again but now she was sitting on a garden wall. I asked her if she was OK. She said that she was lost, that her old labrador had just retired after a lifetime's service and that the new dog they'd given her was useless.

Then she said, 'Anyway, are you OK, love? You smell like you've been in a fire.'

I told her what had happened and walked her home. The dog sniffed at the blood on my shoes, then gave me a look.

When I got home I had another cup of tea and fed Alfredo, my little dog. Then I soldered in the new capacitor, set the timer, and bingo, the damn thing blew my fucking arms off.

Perfect Crime

Elvis borrowed a book of suicides from the Forensic Pathology section. It was a short loan and it pleased him to think that he would be dead before it was due back. Back in his apartment he studied it like it was the Sears Catalogue, but which one to choose? They were all successful methods or they wouldn't have been in the book.

Prison suicides, where the wonderful power of the human spirit, which people were always talking about, turned nasty on itself. Inmates cutting short their sentences in desperately ingenious ways. The man who put a dessert spoon handle-first into his nose and brought his head sharply down on to a table, or another who inserted a mop-pole into his rectum and jumped backwards off a chair.

Some solutions to his little problem were only available to those with the fortitude and determination of the completely insane, like the eleven-centimetre nail which one man succeeded in driving into his brain with a mallet, or the woman patient who had simply forced her head into a washbasin, breathed deeply, and drowned.

One of the points made in the book was that in some ways suicide could be seen as a perfect crime; an unlawful act which requires courage and ingenuity. The idea appealed to him and he contemplated his own death with this in mind, no longer content to just pick one out of the book, intent now on something original, effective and painless, something to be remembered by.

He made the down-payment on a beautiful 30.06 Remington Gamemaster hunting rifle, complete with a Shilba 4 × 15 coated image telescopic sight. He knew a telescopic sight was unnecessary, but the man at Gun Mart and Sporting Goods was so helpful that he bought it anyway. After all, he had the address on the credit agreement, he'd get it all back soon enough.

Elvis did not wish the sound of the rifle to be the last thing he heard, in fact he was afraid of the noise made by guns. He didn't want to be discovered with his face contorted by fear as it would be if he heard the cartridge explode in the chamber.

The solution, he decided, was to shoot himself while he was unconscious – he already had plenty of tranquillisers. He held the muzzle of the rifle steady in a rubber collar made from a hot-water bottle, fixed around his neck with insulation tape. To pull the trigger he used the mechanism from an electric alarm clock which he bought from K-mart.

Elvis loaded and cocked the rifle, set the clock and swallowed the tranquillisers. He settled back in his chair. The clock was only a cheap two-jewel model but it would suffice.

Elvis and His Mom Were Lovers

It was shoddy, very shoddy, the way the pageant
treated me.

Death stole his dream of hosting Miss America just
one more time.

Outrageous rumours say he fathered a black baby.

Scars on his back – whipped for not picking enough
cotton.

A blue-collar construction worker who definitely
doesn't like blacks. He likes to drink beer, he's
going to wear cowboy boots . . .

During one unguarded moment I told them what
they wanted to hear, and it was all true.

Still, being the man he was, he tried to hold his
family together.

He thought this girl was his mom – back from the dead.

She got very mean when she was drinking. And when she took those diet pills and drank too, it was really scary.

The rain fell harder, big splashing drops.

All he had was a radio and a guitar.

Diary of Larry Geller, Elvis's Hairdresser and Spiritual Guide

Yesterday morning I witnessed a shocking spectacle. Twenty dead bodies of men, women and children were brought to Graceland as a present from the folks over in Nashville. They were distributed among the guys and their families to be cooked and eaten. They were dragged about on the terrace and into the pool. The children amused themselves by sporting with and mutilating the body of a little girl. A crowd of men and women maltreated the body of a grey-haired old man and that of a young woman. By this time human entrails had formed a thick crust on the surface of the pool, completely blocking the filter. Mutilated limbs, heads and trunks were floating about, and scenes of horror were presented to our view in every direction. How true it is that the dark places of the earth are full of the habitations of cruelty.

This morning a little after the break of day I was surprised to hear the voices of several persons who were talking very loudly near the music gates. On going out to ascertain the cause of the noise, I found a human head in the garden. This was the head of an old man which Elvis had left there the night before to annoy the staff. It was the head of the same old guy who had been abused so cruelly on the terrace yesterday. The arm of the body had been broken by a bullet from Elvis's .38 which had passed through the bone near the shoulder, and the upper part of the skull had been knocked off with a baseball bat.

One of the servants of the King ran away a few months ago. She was soon captured by the police and brought back to Graceland. Then, at Elvis's command, her arm was cut off below the elbow and cooked for the King who ate it in her presence, then ordered that her body be burned in different parts. The girl, who against all the odds grew to be a woman and is still living, wrote a book entitled *Elvis Ate my Right Arm*, which to date has sold over two million copies.

Last week Elvis had two battle-fatigued dudes shipped over from Vietnam. He soon discovered they were very scared and docile and that he could do as he pleased with them. He told them that they were to be killed just as soon there was nothing good on TV.

'That is very cruel,' said one of them. 'If you allow us to live I will give you my canoe.'

'Keep your fucking canoe,' said Elvis, 'I want to eat men.'

Directly after *Hawaii Five-O* had finished the cruel deed was perpetrated. The two boys doomed to die were made to dig a hole in the earth for the purpose of making a native oven, and were then required to cut firewood to roast their own bodies. They were then directed to take a shower and afterwards to make a cup out of a banana-leaf; this, from opening a vein in each boy's arm was soon filled with blood. This blood was then drunk, in the presence of the sufferers, by the Kamba people.

Elvis then had their arms cut off, cooked and eaten, some of the flesh being presented to them. He then ordered a fish-hook to be put into their tongues, which were then drawn out as far as possible before being cut off. These were barbecued and eaten to taunts of 'We are eating your tongues!' As the life of the victims was still not extinct, an incision was made in the side of each man and his bowels ripped out. This soon terminated their sufferings in this world.

I feel like I'm partly responsible really. I talk to Elvis about spirituality while I'm cutting his hair and for a while now I've been encouraging him to investigate other cultures and to embrace their customs and belief systems. Usually people just get into meditation, do a little yoga, maybe have some acupuncture and burn a few joss-sticks. But not this. How the fuck was I to know it would turn out this way and that the fat fool and his friends would start eating people? Elvis already eats far too damn much as it is.

An Amazing Talk with Elvis

I know a lot of people think I'm a kook, but I was up there on the ceiling, watching them work on me. When they put the shocks on my chest, my body jumped up. I heard this ringing noise, brrrrrnnnnng-brrrrrnnnnng-brrrrrrnnnnng, very rhythmic. Then I was moving through this – you're going to think I'm a kook too – through this long dark place. It seemed like a sewer or something. I just can't describe it to you. I was moving, beating all the time with this noise, this ringing noise. I felt like I was drawn through a limited area, a kind of funnel I guess. It was dark and black in there, and I moved through it quickly, back to my body. And as I started being sucked back, it seemed like the suction started from the head, like I went into the head. I didn't feel like I had any say-so about it at all, nor even time to think about it. I was there, yards away from my body, and all of a sudden it was over with. I didn't even have time to think, I'm being sucked back into my body.

Of all the girls you've read about, there was only one

I really cared for. The girl I met in Guam, remember –
the girl in the pictures, saying goodbye to me?

After we said goodbye I had this experience that I
was giving birth to a child. The delivery was very
difficult, and I lost a lot of blood. The doctor gave me
up, and told my relatives that I was dying. However, I
was quite alert through this whole thing, and even as I
heard him saying this I felt myself coming to. As I did, I
realised that all these people were there, almost in
multitudes it seems, hovering around the ceiling of the
room. They were all the people I had known in my past
life, the Colonel was there, and Roy Orbison and Joe
Esposito were there too.

I recognised my grandmother and a girl I had known
when I was in school, and many other relatives and
friends. It seems that I mainly saw their faces and felt
their presence. They all seemed pleased. It was a very
happy occasion, and I felt that they had come to
protect or to guide me. It was almost as if I were
coming home, and they were there to greet or to
welcome me. All this time, I had the feeling of everything light and beautiful. It was a beautiful and glor-
ious moment.

I've changed a lot since I was in my teens.

An Amazing Talk with Elvis: Part Two

Max and I checked into the barracks when we got to Germany, but after preliminaries I was put on a bus and taken to an isolated place eight miles outside the base. There were six L-shaped barracks set up inside a high electrified fence with barbed wire at the top. Inside the compound there was a movie theatre, a store, a barbershop, a chow hall, and a recreation centre. There were several hundred guys living in that compound.

I was strapped down in the bed. I was yelling and screaming about something. I'm not the type of person that cusses that much. I hardly ever use foul language, but I know that I said some pretty foul things to those men who were with me. But after I woke up in the hospital I was not resentful. I was passive. I lay there thinking, trying to recall the last memories I had before I woke up in that bed. I didn't remember anything. It was like I'd been asleep for my entire life up to that point.

They told me I wasn't in Germany any more; while I was knocked out they'd flown me to Guam. They showed me a Western Union telegram, it had my name on it and a whole row of numbers. Then they told me I had a special assignment.

I met a girl called Pat. We hit it off from the start. We had the same interests, we were nervous about the same things, and we would laugh at the same kind of jokes. We were two individuals who were very very close, and where one lacked a quality, the other had something that filled that lack.

I'd talk to the other guys in the service and they'd talk about getting laid in Hong Kong or Japan or Korea. I didn't have to talk about anything. I didn't have to brag. I'd just smile at them, secure in my love for Pat.

Two months before my tour of duty was meant to expire, I was sent home. Pat stayed behind at the base. We exchanged home addresses, but somehow I lost hers and now I can't remember her last name, or even the town she came from. I never saw her again.

Pat was a liberated woman, she knew exactly who she was. And that's just the kind of woman I like to be around. She fulfilled every need I had to such a degree that it's a problem now. I can't meet a girl that's as good as she was. When you've been in paradise, it's hard to find paradise again. You always want to go back.

I think of her all the time, but I just can't remember her last name. It's a total blank. I just can't remember.

When I first got out of the service, all I could remember about my four years was that I'd had a lot of fun . . . I mean all the pictures I have, and all the recollections I had, were of Pat and I having fun, skin-diving, laying on the beach, collecting shells, walking in the jungle. It never dawned on me until later that I must have *done* something while I was in the service.

An Amazing Talk with Elvis: Part Three

I would like to state for the record that I believe that the United States Air Force was always extremely fair to me in my military career. I enjoyed my military career and consider myself to be a loyal member of the United States Air Force, retired.

When it came time to get processed out, I wanted to get the medals I earned while stationed in Germany. They were actually theatre ribbons. I had so many ribbons when I left the base that the officer I reported to told me not to wear them because I would attract attention to myself.

During the out-processing they brought out my file. They do that regularly every year anyway. They show you your records and have you go over them and make sure that they're correct. Then you sign a paper that states the records have been approved by you. The last time I was shown my records, they'd been changed. Instead of all the typed dog-eared reports that were in my file before, there was this clean computer print-out.

I asked the officer in charge what had happened to the notices of me being awarded those theatre ribbons. He told me that since I had such a high security clearance some of the things in my files made it necessary to expunge a lot of the information from the record. He said that there was a top-secret file on me which was available to people who had the right clearances. The file he had me approve was the one which would be shown to anyone who did not have the highest clearance. He said that was because this was more or less a public record, and it could not have anything on it of a sensitive nature. It was very misleading, that report. It looked like I had been a supply man, a box pusher, and I'd done nothing else, except try to attempt suicide. The phony hospital story was in the report, so deniability was built in.

One guy would ask me questions in an accusatory manner. Another guy would come over and say comforting things. Then the first guy would come back and accuse me again. Then the second guy would come and pat my arm and be friendly. I can remember their faces and their tone of voice, but I can't remember the content of what they were talking about.

Then I went through the normal out-processing and

went home. All I can say is that everybody, my folks, my friends, everyone who'd known me before, noticed how changed I was. I was fearful, and under tight control.

An Amazing Talk with Elvis: Part Four

At my first job interview I was asked to fill out the company's routine job application form. I wrote my name and then I noticed that my hands were sweating. As I began to enter my address my heart was pounding so loudly it was audible. I fought to remain calm, but within a few moments I grabbed the form and bolted out of the door.

Next day I went to another interview. Again I was asked to fill out a job application. This time I got further in filling out the form; name . . . address . . . Social Security number . . . health information . . . but when I came to the place in the form which required work information about the past four years, the pounding in my ears, the shortness of breath, and the terrifying feeling of being confined in a small space came over me again, and I left the building with the form wadded up in my hand.

Over the next few months I applied for many more jobs. The results were always the same. The mere mention of computers made me fly into a rage. I still couldn't face whatever it was that was blocking me. To this day I can't stand the thought of a computer. I'd like to smash them all up.

One day I had a vivid dream. Then it was like, little by little, memory cells exploding in my brain. I began to remember certain incidents. At first I didn't know if these were real memories or just dreams. Today, I still don't know if they are accurate or not, but they are so real in all their details that I believe they are the truth.

I believe I'm telling the truth, and I'd like to see someone disprove it. I only have these fragments of memory, so if I went to the Air Force they'd pull out my folder and throw it on the desk and say, 'See, there it is in black and white . . . He's a nut. He tried to commit suicide by taking a patent medicine.'

I feel I was used. Why would they use an enlisted man who was supposed to be a supply man? Every squadron has supply personnel, so I guess it's perfect cover. A supply man is so common he wouldn't be noticed. How well it worked out, from their point of view, I just don't know. But from mine, well, it didn't work out too well. All the doubts and fears I have now, years later, and after a lot of psychiatric help, which I paid for myself, made the experiment, if it was one, a failure to me.

I never thought about laying down my life, in fact the Colonel told me the whole deal was just for morale, that the worst I'd have to do was shave off my side-burns, but maybe I laid down a lot more than my life in the service of my country.

Stairway to Heaven

Elvis opened up the throttle and felt his brand new Jetstar surge forwards along the runway. As he eased back the stick the plane's nose came up and the rumble of tyres on tarmac was replaced by the low whistle of wind across wings and fuselage. He was airborne and he felt great. There was a dull clunk as the under-carriage folded away and Elvis tuned the radio to Country Roads FM. He punched in a course for Cleveland, Ohio and hit the autopilot switch. Then he cracked open a Pepsi and washed down a handful of pills.

A few months earlier when he was on tour, Elvis met Led Zeppelin on the tarmac of LA International Airport. Elvis hated Led Zeppelin. He called them 'long-haired British freaks'. He hated their music, he hated their lyrics, he hated their album covers, he hated the way they looked, he hated the way they talked. He despised everything they stood for. Elvis's stepbrothers, David and Ricky Stanley, aged seventeen and eighteen, were along for the ride. Both huge Zep fans, they'd wear Led Zeppelin T-shirts just to annoy Elvis, and when they saw their heroes disembarking from a nearby plane they dragged Elvis over with them so they had an excuse to meet the band.

Robert Plant, Jimmy Page, John Paul Jones and John Bonham all signed autographs for the two boys who by this time had entered their own private Heavy Metal Heaven, and as they stood talking, Elvis looked over at their jet.

'I like your 707.'

'Yeah?' said Robert Plant. 'We lease it from—'

'Oh?' Elvis interrupted. 'I *own* mine.' Robert looked a little surprised at this, but he let it go and there was a short embarrassed silence.

'My kid brothers tell me you guys are pretty heavy,' Elvis said, desperately trying to plug the gaping hole he'd just ripped out of the conversation.

'Yeah, but not as heavy as you, you fat fuck,' replied Plant, trying to be funny, as only the British know how.

'OK, guys, that's it . . . we're leaving!' Elvis screamed, and stormed back across the blacktop to his own jet. Then he cancelled the gig and took off for Memphis. The trip back was a nightmare, the plane lost an engine on takeoff, made a very rough emergency landing at an airport in Burbank and Elvis was forced to abandon the remainder of his tour.

Convinced that Led Zeppelin had sabotaged his plane, Elvis was now on his way to teach them a lesson.

As his jet approached the outskirts of Cleveland, Elvis switched back to manual control and, retuning the radio to 'Those Were the Days' FM, he cranked the volume up as high as it would go. Then, with the 'March of the Dambusters' blasting away in his head-set and all kinds of prescription chemicals coursing through his veins, he jammed the stick forwards. The plane plummeted to 500 feet and levelled out over the Jacobs Field baseball park where a Led Zep gig was in full force. By now Elvis was so excited that his whole body was quivering. It was the point in the show where the band leave drummer John Bonham alone on the stage to perform his obligatory twenty-minute solo. The Jetstar came in fast and low over the field and with trembling hands Elvis inched back the two small levers which operated the cargo doors. He'd loaded up the hold of the Jetstar with large polythene garbage sacks filled with a mixture of water, pigs' blood and food dye. Then he'd shat in them all for good measure. The doors swung open and the whole bloody, shitty pay-load slithered out into the skies of Cleveland – directly over the auditorium. The crowd roared with approval:

Led Zeppelin were acknowledged masters of spectacle and their audience not only expected them to deliver – each time it had to be bigger and better. Unfortunately for the massed heavy metal fans gathered below, several hours of high-altitude flying had frozen the liquid-filled sacks into solid lumps of ice which shattered on impact. The result was total and instantaneous carnage. Shards of red ice ripped through the crowd carving out long bloody corridors all the way to the stage and at the high point of his solo the neatly severed head of a young woman bounced off John Bonham's snare and lodged itself inside the PA.

As his plane climbed rapidly to five thousand feet Elvis was oblivious to what was happening below; he thought he'd just played the best practical joke in the whole history of practical jokes ever, and he was laughing like a demented hyena. Backstage, the band decided it was time to forget about love, peace and harmony for a while. So far the body count was estimated at 30 and rising by the minute, with a further 220 fans seriously injured. It was already the worst disaster in Cleveland since the river caught fire. Shouting above the wail of sirens and the throb of paramedic helicopters, a badly shaken Robert Plant began to make a few phone calls.

Darkness had fallen by the time an elated Elvis touched down in Memphis. As he drove his Lincoln back home from the airstrip he heard the dull 'crump' of what he recognised from his army days to be a parachute mine, exploding somewhere in the distance. As he swung the car off Elvis Presley Boulevard, through the music gates and up the gravel drive towards Graceland, Elvis thought that the house looked somehow different. Then he realised that the upper floors were gone. Just like his birthplace in Tupelo, Graceland was now a bungalow. The shattered trees of the Meditation Garden were festooned with clothing and broken chandeliers. Splintered furniture and chunks of masonry littered the lawns.

Elvis found Ricky and David crouching in the bushes by the pool house. Both seriously injured, they weren't making too much sense, but they managed to tell him that Priscilla was still inside the house. He raced towards the front entrance and, pushing through the debris in what remained of the lobby, he started up the main staircase. He saw then that it was shorn clean away and that now the stairway just vanished into the starry heavens. Then something made him stop short.

Looking up, he saw Priscilla spreadeagled across the first flight. Her face, wide open from scalp to chin, had no connection with anything that Elvis had ever seen.

Jungle Room

I'm sat in the jungle room with Elvis and my brother Red. Elvis is just back from his de-tox at the Baptist Hospital; he's got a big tour coming up so we're keeping an eye on him. We're watching some crappy daytime TV gameshow. First prize is a hostess trolley, a big hand and a fluffy red bunny-rabbit.

'Item,' mutters Elvis, 'the said Agnes Sampson was again brought before the King's majesty and his Council, and being examined of the meetings and detestable dealings of those witches, she confessed that on the night of All-Hallows Eve last, she was accompanied not only by the aforesaid witches, but a great many other witches also, to the number of two hundred; and that they all together went by sea, each one in a riddle or sieve, and went in the same riddles or sieves very substantially with the flagons of wine making merry and drinking by the way, until they reached the church of the sacred heart in Loma Linda; and after that they had landed, they joined hands on the front lawn and danced this reel or short dance singing all with one voice,

'We hope yer bleedin' chandeliers catch fire'.

At which time, she confessed, Dr Flan did go before them playing this reel or dance upon a small trump, called a Jew's trump, until they entered the church of the sacred heart . . .'

'Item,' says Elvis again, 'the said Agnes Sampson confessed that the Devil being then in Loma Linda awaiting their arrival in the likeness of a man, and seeing that they tarried overlong, he enjoined them all to do a penance, which was that they should kiss his buttocks, as a sign of their duty to him, which being put over the rail of the altar, everyone did as he had enjoined them.

'The Devil appeared in the pulpit. He was a little black man, velvet suit, lace cuffs, hundreds of shiny white teeth, gold rings on his fingers and oil all in his hair. He looked a lot like Sammy Davis Jnr. He had a black book in his hand from which he called out the name of every one of the hits of Frankie Avalon, desiring all in attendance to be good servants to him. Frankie then appeared in miniaturised form inside a tiny ball of fire above the altar, and those who handled him said his body was hard like iron; his face was terrible, his nose like the beak of an eagle, great burning eyes; his arms and legs were hairy, with claws upon his hands and feet like a griffon.'

I turn to my brother Red.

'Has that fat motherfucker been at the pills again?'

He glances over at the King of Rock 'n' Roll, hero and role-model to teenagers the world over. Elvis is slumped in a chair, Christ knows what going on inside his head, saliva trickling from one corner of his mouth . . .

Red grins.

'Are bears Catholic? Does the Pope shit in the woods? Course he fuckin' has.'

Well, I do declare, my kid brother Red. He is one comical bastard.

Lansky Brothers

In March 1956 Elvis bought a red and black Fleetwood reg. 56007. In August of that year Elvis exchanged the car for a wardrobe of clothes with his
friend Bernard Lansky, owner of Lansky Bros. Lanskys specialised in loud clothing . . . yellow suits, pink
sports coats, and white shoes.

The shop, a former army surplus store, was taken
over and refitted by Bernard in 1939 and catered
mainly to black patrons, including Rufus Thomas
and Junior Parker. Elvis first shopped there in 1952,
and afterwards bought clothing from there for many
years. Many of the Sun recording artists, notably Roy
Orbison, also bought their clothes at Lanskys.

Bernard was born in Berlin. His father, Frederick, had
originally been a kosher butcher, but in the early 1920s
his wife died and soon afterwards his business failed.
Bernard and his brother Hubert were packed off to the
country to stay with Frederick's childless sister and
their once-prosperous father was reduced to selling

hot-dogs at one of the railway stations in Berlin. He was a thin, insignificant man with a haggard face and a sloping moustache. About twice a month he used to spend a day on the platform where long-distance slow trains with cheap, fourth-class carriages stopped. If he saw a girl getting out of one of these carriages who looked as if she was coming to the city to find a job as a housemaid, and if she was fat enough, he would approach her, politely lift his cap and enquire whether he could be of any assistance. During the conversation he would slip in a remark that he was in need of a housekeeper for his bachelor household and that she could have the job if she wanted it. He'd say that he paid well and that there was not too much work for her to do anyway. Often a girl accepted, and any who did would not be seen again.

Frederick would employ each of these girls for a couple of days and then murder them. He cut up the bodies with a butcher's skill, kept the flesh and disposed of the balance in the sewer. Then he pickled the meat, ground it to a pulp and put it into the sausages which he later sold at the railway station. The constant stream of girls into his flat eventually alerted the neighbours who put the police on his track. Frederick finally confessed when bundles of women's clothes were discovered in the closets.

His sons knew nothing of the case until their father's

trial, and subsequent death sentence, were plastered across the front pages of every newspaper in Germany. Frederick had clearly been driven insane by grief and failure, but in those ugly times he reflected the popular mood and was portrayed in the press as a repellant little Jewish monster. His death was the first of many. Later Bernard and Hubert moved back to Berlin and set themselves up as tailors, cutting, tacking and stitching in the same small apartment where their father had pulverised his hapless victims.

Despite his exuberant appearance Bernard was a quiet and very private man. He'd fled Berlin soon after the horrors of Crystal Night in November 1938, and he eventually set up shop in Memphis, manufacturing and selling the same gaudy clothes he'd seen in so many gangster movies, and his business prospered. Hubert was not so lucky, Bernard had not heard from him since 1939 and he began to fear the worst. In 1945 the International Red Cross contacted Bernard to confirm that his brother's body had been found with hundreds of other Jews at Westerbork concentration camp. Bernard had a signwriter paint 'Lansky Brothers' above his new shop in Hubert's memory.

There had always been rumours about Bernard. Stories of sorcery and malefice, although in a predominantly redneck town like Memphis it was inevitable that a German Jew who wore flashy clothes and ran a thriving business should provoke a certain amount of hostility. Bernard was not unduly worried by the rumours, he was accustomed to the background hum of racial and religious intolerance and most days he just considered himself extremely lucky to be alive.

Eventually the stories gained in bulk and detail to such an extent that sooner or later someone had to bring matters to a head. This occurred in July 1959 when the pastor of the Morah Baptist Church informed the local authorities that a fifteen-year-old boy, Erick Erikssen, had accused Bernard Lansky of kidnapping a number of children in order to hand them over to the Devil.

Bernard was taken into custody and interrogated. A number of other men and women were also implicated by Erick's accusation and the pastor's testimony. All of them declared that they were not guilty, except one elderly woman of seventy-five who confessed to everything. Every single charge that was brought before her was met with the same response. She'd smile sweetly and say, 'Oh yes, I did that, dear, it was the Jew Bernard's idea to give the little ones over to Satan but it was always left to me to do his bidding.'

This was the first time that any concrete form had been given to the rumours and, because of the denunciations and particularly the guilty plea of the lunatic old lady, it began to appear that there might be something in these stories. Soon interest in the case ceased to become regional, and when the supermarket tabloids got hold of the story, and sniffed out Satanic Jewish blood, all hell broke loose.

The laws operating in Tennessee relating to sorcery and malefice at that time were the fairest and most lenient of all such laws in the Southern States. The accused were permitted to ask a local dignitary of their own choosing to preside over the commission of enquiry. The prosecution had to produce at least six witnesses before a charge could be proceeded with, and even if these witnesses could be found, the accused could still escape conviction if they could find twelve witnesses prepared to swear that their character was such that they could not be a witch.

Bernard elected that Elvis would preside over his trial which was scheduled to take place in the open air on an empty plot of land behind the Meditation Garden at Graceland. It was a disaster in the making.

In his mandate to his commissioners, and in a rare moment of clarity, Elvis stipulated that their first endeavour would to be to bring about the rehabilitation of the alleged witches by prayer. The accused were not to be tortured, and wherever possible prison sentences were to be avoided.

Unhappily, this approach did more harm than good, for it seemed merely to encourage an outbreak of mass hysteria. When the commission held its first session on 13 August 1959, a crowd of twenty-three thousand souls gathered at Graceland in order to hear the prayers and exhortations, and to help in the 'discovery' of the witches.

The commission first interrogated the children involved, and when they had heard their evidence they ordered no fewer than seventy persons to be apprehended as witches. Realising that, in the face of such evil, prayers would be utterly ineffectual, the commission decided to apply the law, and as a result twenty-three who, it was maintained, had voluntarily confessed, were sentenced to death, their execution by burning being carried out within a fortnight.

Forty-seven others were also found guilty, and they were burned later in a parking lot across the street. But the most hideous feature of the case was the burning of fifteen children aged between nine and eleven. Thirty-six other children, whose degree of guilt was found to be less than that of those who burned, were sentenced to run the gauntlet, and to be caned on their hands at the church door in Morah, once a week for a year. Fifteen others, who were all under nine, were to receive the same punishment on three successive Sundays.

They saved Bernard's trial until last, and it soon became obvious that he stood absolutely no chance of escaping with his life. Anyone who tried to speak up in his defence was immediately branded as being in league with the Devil and then taken into custody. There was really nothing anybody could have done to help him and such was the level of hysteria that even Elvis was powerless.

Bernard had travelled all the way from Hitler's murderous Germany to be in America, Land of the extremely Brave and of the very fucking Free, to get himself far away from exactly this kind of superstitious medieval shit and now he found himself in precisely the same situation he would have faced if he'd just stayed home. He was definitely going to die.

Bernard spent his last night in one of the guest rooms at Graceland. After spending several hours talking with Elvis he retired and he tried to rest. He could not dispel the horror of the coming morning so he sat up and prayed. He thought about his life, of the miles he'd covered in his quest to be happy, to be left alone and in the meantime to earn an honest living, of his dead mother and father and of his poor brother Hubert, murdered by the Nazis. Eventually he felt ready to lie down, but not for long. At 6 a.m. he decided that it was useless and dressed carefully in his flashiest clothes, a lavender safari jacket, flared white pants and a lemon-yellow shirt. He tied a polyester stars-and-stripes scarf around his neck and polished his best snakeskin boots to an unbearable sheen.

Elvis personally cooked Bernard a breakfast of fried banana sandwiches and biscuits with maple syrup, then brewed him a pot of fresh coffee. He attended a short service which Elvis had organised for him in his private chapel at Graceland. Then Bernard spent fifteen minutes alone among the flowers of the Meditation Garden. His open grave was barely screened from his view. He watched the sun come up over Memphis for the very last time and took in the rose-scented air. He would soon be reunited with his family, and he would die like a gentleman.

The hanging party came for him and pinioned his arms. Elvis was present too and accompanied the hurried procession to the drop. Bernard Lansky almost ran towards it. They slipped a clean white hood over his head and fastened the noose tightly under his chin. He sensed the executioner step aside, heard the snap of the lever, and felt himself fall the first few inches of the seven-foot four-inch drop.

From Elvis's Secret Diary

Will anyone believe this story?

Not unless they have seen the things which I have seen.

A woman wrote to me and I arranged to meet her in a Covent Garden cafe.

She was in a deplorable condition.

Emaciated, wild-eyed and twitching.

Normal for London in other words.

Concealed behind Nottingham lace curtains in a mean street north of the river was a beautiful little temple of the greater mysteries.

Very soon curious things began to happen. We became most desperately afflicted with black cats. They were not hallucinatory cats, they were so cute and fluffy and lover-ly and every day we were engaged in pushing loads of them off our doorstep with a big fat stick. We had never seen so many, nor such dreadful specimens. The whole house was filled with the horrible stench of the brutes. Every day I went to my studio in the city where I design party clothes for rich midgets, and found that, too, was filled with the penetrating reek of tom-cat.

Coming upstairs after breakfast one morning, I suddenly saw, coming down the stairs towards me, a gigantic tabby cat, twice the size of a tiger.

I dialled 666, phoned the occult police, but I got their answering-machine instead. 'Please call back later,' it said, 'we're a bit busy right now.'

Useless bunch of bastards.

From Elvis's Secret Diary:
Part Two

Miss X was from London.

   She lived almost exclusively on uncooked vegetarian foods.

Had I been older and wiser I should have recognised a pathology of an emotional nature in which the sex instinct takes the form of an impulse to inflict pain.

   At the time I knew she was verging on a breakdown.

An assembly of blear-eyed people complaining of disturbed nights.

Waked from a nightmare, I struggled with a weight on my chest.

Even after consciousness had fully returned, the room seemed full of EVIL.

Presently, up to an open window came another member of our community, a woman who, like her, ate only uncooked vegetarian foods and

STANK SO BADLY OF SHIT,

that she slept in an open-air shelter, some little distance downwind of our house.

The same nightmare.

The village baker's version of war bread.

She had conceived a crush on me. I give them scant politeness.

Whatever may be the rights and wrongs of the case, I had roused her resentment in good earnest. That afternoon I was afflicted by the most vivid and shocking dream I have ever had in my life.

Waking from sleep, I saw distinctly the head of Miss X, reduced to the size of an orange, floating in the air at the foot of my bed and snapping its teeth at me.

It was the most malignant thing I have ever seen.

I popped into The Angling Man, 112–116 Narborough Road, Leicester.

I bought fifty yards of two pound breaking strain monofilament, a pack of twenty Number 18 barbless eyed hooks and two pints of cherry-red eosin maggots. I reckoned the rain that was forecast for that night would make the water fairly muddy but the bream would probably still be able to pick out a red maggot.

As groundbait is not allowed in the lake where I fish, I use a Peter Drenann medium swimfeeder and I always put it on a weak link just in case it gets snagged. I like to cast on a five-spot pattern and fill in with the catapult, and so for this I got a pound of mixed hemp and tares and a pint and a half of castors. You don't want to feed with the same stuff you use on the hook, bland and bulk is best for the feeder, that way the hook-bait presents itself as more of a delicacy.

Anyway, next morning the storm broke.

Miss X and I were peacefully at work in the kitchen when she suddenly caught up a carving knife and started after me, mad as a March hare. Fortunately for me I had in my hands a large saucepan full of freshly boiled hemp and tares, and I used this as a weapon of defence. As we danced around the kitchen table, slopping hot bland swimfeeder water in all directions, she slashed at me with the knife. I cornered her by the sink and brought the saucepan down on her head with a satisfying thud. I do sincerely hope I put that bitch in the hospital for a very long time.

I did pretty well that day. I got twenty-seven pounds of bream, a couple of really nice tench and also a six-pound carp, which is no big deal by specialist standards, but it's a lovely bonus if you can manage to land one on light tackle.

Fame & Fortune

He goes into the bathroom with a favourite book, *Cheiro's Book of Numbers*, his finger stuck into it as a marker. He glances at himself in the mirror. Blue pyjamas. Puffy eyes and face. Bad colour.

He sits down in a wicker chair by the tub, staring at the open book in his lap, his eyes glassy, his body motionless. His big body slumps imperceptibly, then shifts and topples out of the chair, the noise of the fall muffled by the thick brown shag carpeting.

Inside the house, just past the National Guardsmen standing at stiff attention at the door, he lies at rest inside a 900-pound copper-lined coffin, beneath a crystal chandelier. He's wearing a white suit, a light blue shirt, and a white tie. His greying sideburns are dyed black, his hair brittle with lacquer and his face coated with a thick skim of embalming cream. Every florist in the city has sold out.

He was a frail human being. He would be the first to admit his weakness. His rapid rise to fame and fortune offered him temptations that most never experience. He would not want anyone to think that he had no flaws or faults.

The caravan, led by a silver Cadillac followed by the white Cadillac hearse with his body and seventeen white Cadillac limousines, rolls slowly down the curving drive on to the main street, and then to the cemetery. A brief ceremony follows in the white marble mausoleum where he is entombed. The huge coffin slides into place. His father stands quietly by it for a moment, then walks slowly away, as workmen enter and begin to cover the opening with concrete.

Alone in its tomb, his body begins to putrefy. The scrotum becomes swollen and discoloured; the abdomen distends as gas builds up inside it. Blood-stained fluid escapes from the mouth and nostrils. Eventually, under the pressure of the gases of putrefaction – sulphuretted hydrogen, carburetted hydrogen, ammonia, carbon dioxide, and phosphoretted hydrogen – the abdominal and thoracic cavities burst open. The nails are shed and the hair loosens. The linings of the trachea and larynx liquify.

Then the eyes dissolve.

Country Song

This is me here, me getting off the bus and being
led away by strange boys, this is me having a drink,
me getting lost later that night.

Two-roomed shotgun house, front porch, bedroom,
back kitchen.

This woman was found dead in her kitchen by her
husband when he returned home from work one
evening. There is an axe on the left side of the
body, a knife on the table and an opened coal gas
stove, the taps of which are turned on. He saw her,
and because of the wound to her head suspected
foul play, but it transpired that she had tried to kill
herself with an axe and tried to stab herself with a
knife. Both of these injuries were trivial and had not
caused her death. She had finally resorted to gassing
herself and death was ultimately due to carbon
monoxide poisoning which was revealed by the high
level of carboxyhaemoglobin in her blood.

This young girl killed herself by applying a 12-gauge shotgun to her forehead and pulling the trigger. The position of the body and the weapon at first sight suggests that the wound may not have been self-inflicted, but it was almost certainly produced by sitting, holding the muzzle of the gun to her forehead and pulling the trigger. When she fell backwards from the force of the explosion the gun recoiled between her legs. In reaching this conclusion I am influenced by the fact that this is a common pattern of suicidal gunshot wounding, though the weapon is often some distance from the fatal wound because of the recoil.

The corpse of a woman lying alongside a pond in the middle of autumn.

The dead body of a man found beside his bed.

A sink full of dirty dishes.

A modern mortuary.

The severely charred body of a man.

A stab-hole in a dress.

The tattooed arm of a drug addict.

One of eleven children born into desperate poverty
in rural Missouri, she was raped at the age of eight
by one of her father's friends. At fifteen she
married.
She bore three sons in four years, then became a
battered wife who eventually collapsed in a nervous
breakdown.

White soul music: the singer as star and victim.

All she had was a radio and a guitar.

Downtown

Elvis and Joe staggered home along the dusty road, heads swimming and eyes squinting in the strong sunlight which was already laying the foundations for a monumental hangover.

They stopped for a breather outside an abandoned clapboard house. At one time it had been let to a retired couple who'd been forced to sell their midtown apartment and use the proceeds plus their life savings to pay for medical treatment. When they'd moved in, destitute and with nowhere else to go, the old lady was recovering from cancer, and the after-effects of the chemotherapy. They'd taken her leg off, cut away half her insides to stop the cancer from spreading, and given her an artificial leg. She'd dragged herself around on it, clinging to the shattered furniture, too scared, old and stubborn to learn how to make the metal limb co-operate with the movements and impulses of the rest of her body.

She never really recovered from what the doctors did to her body to make her well again and when she died, three years later, her husband had disappeared. One of the landlord's men came and boarded the place up until it could be re-let, and it had stood peeling and empty ever since.

Pushing their way into the tangled front yard, they stumbled through a waist-high forest of ragwort buzzing with insects and teeming with thousands of black and yellow cinnabar moth caterpillars.

The boards came away easily enough from the rotted frame around the back door, and they found themselves in the kitchen. All they had to do then was to push the windows open, the shuttering fell away, and there was light.

The kitchen was exactly as it had been left a year before. Everything was covered in a fine grey powder, a bitter smell of decay filled the room. Every step raised a puff of dust around their legs. Regimented tins of food still stood in the cupboards, but the milk carton by the stove seemed to contain a cocktail of putty and livid green bile. Books and magazines were stacked neatly on the dresser, and a coat hung behind the back door.

The parlour was dominated by a monstrous china cabinet, grey marble-effect Formica with black plastic trim, and gold sailing ships painted on its curving glass doors. On top a collection of dry stalks sticking out of plant pots, all carefully placed on neat lace coasters. In the dark, not even the cacti had survived. A pair of tartan carpet slippers sat on the rug by the sofa. On a side table two little fish floated belly-up in a half-empty glass bowl. Their eyes were glazed over with a translucent white film, patches of orange scales glinting through the fluffy grey fungus which engulfed their bloated bodies.

Elvis and Joe pushed through a curtain into the tiny lean-to bedroom. The metal leg was lying on the bed, its leather gaiter hanging open like a trap, unbuckled from the stump before they took her corpse away. A greasy impression on the sheets showed the way the body had lain. Her teeth were still in a glass by the bed, like some hideous specimen from a pathology museum, bleached cretaceous white by twelve months' immersion in Denti-kleen. Under the tangle of dead hairs on the pillow, a dark stain spread out from where her mouth had been.

Noline

The new minister's appeal had made such an impression on Bob that he determined to try to influence someone to join the choir and accept Christ. Bob's home was about five miles from the public high school he attended. Riding the school bus, he had become well acquainted with his schoolmates who rode the same bus.

Elvis and Joe admitted later that they had not been much interested in joining a church choir, but because Bob had seemed like such a gullible self-righteous young man, they thought that by going along they might be able to have some fun with him. The two boys were not fascinated by the sermon that was preached that evening, nor did they enjoy the choir and the over-friendliness of the other members, nor any of the other happy-clappy shit which they had to sit through. Later on when they led Bob away down an alley, tied him to a metal grille and took turns in sodomising his lifeless body, they had to admit that religion was indeed a good thing and that the church would provide them with an active Christian experience, enabling them to look to the future with full faith and confidence.

Matthew Atkins was not sure, as yet, that he wanted to become a member of the church. But Elvis and Joe encouraged him to keep on attending the series of meetings. Even by the time the series ended, Matthew was still undecided. But he had enjoyed singing in the choir and was willing to continue his participation in the regular church services. Elvis and Joe were both praying earnestly that Matthew would be able to see the advantage of building his personal philosophy around a religious faith.

One evening, while the three boys were together, Matthew said, 'As you both know, I have been doing a lot of thinking about religion. I have watched the enjoyment that you both seem to have attained in life without engaging in foolish entertainments or having to waste a lot of money, and I believe that your way is best after all. I just don't know how to be religious, but if you will show me the way, I would like to come along with you and become a member of your church.'

Joe slipped the cord from his dressing gown and wound it around Matthew's neck, Elvis took a hobbies knife and jammed it into Matthew's chest, just over the sterno-clavicular articulation of the left clavicle. The blade, which was only three-quarters of an inch long, entered the common carotid artery. Death was practically instantaneous.

John David was not opposed to religion, he simply didn't have time for it. He was interested in machinery, automobiles and motorcycles. In addition he was daring and adventuresome. He owned a motorcycle, and his friends chided him for being very reckless in its use. He did not fear danger, and he received a great thrill from accomplishing feats with the motorcycle that others dare not attempt.

One day John lent his motorcycle to a classmate. This friend was a serious-minded boy who had taken a personal interest in religion and who was consistent in his activities and therefore respected by all his friends. This boy was cautious and trustworthy. But in the course of his trip on the borrowed motorcycle it suddenly became necessary to avoid a car. In doing so the motorcycle hit an obstruction, and the boy was thrown for many feet. His head struck a tree and the accident ended fatally.

This circumstance brought about a total change in John David's life. He seemed to recognise that in the experience the Lord had a personal message for him.

He kept asking the question, 'Why is it that I have been spared and my friend has been permitted to die?' This question finally forced him to the conclusion that his friend was ready to die and that the Lord had spared his own life for a purpose.

So John turned over a new leaf.

He surrendered his life to the Lord's leading.

He retained his vigour and zest.

He used his energies in profitable directions.

He pointed himself towards a life of unselfish service.

He found greater satisfaction.

He joined Elvis and Joe's choir and Bible class.

In John's case an examination of the scene made it clear that the assault had been rather a prolonged one. The attack, which had commenced at the entrance to his house, had been continued along the passage and in the kitchen. The instrument of attack had been a wooden curtain pole. Human tissue was present on the floor of the passage, on a leaf of the kitchen table, on the walls, and on the gilt frame of a picture. Several of the pieces showed attached hair and, in addition, hairs were adherent to different articles. A comparison between these specimens and the hair on what remained of John's head showed that all were generally consistent with a common source. Blood-staining, which was copious and diffuse, was present on the front door of the house, in the passage, and in the kitchen.

John survived for some twenty-eight hours. His injuries, which for the greater part involved the posterior half of the scalp, over an area of seven by six inches, were lacerated in character. Multiple wounds were present, and the majority which extended to bone had caused separation of the scalp tissues from the skull. Considerable areas of scalp tissue were missing from where the skull had been denuded of tissue. Other lacerated wounds were present on the face, and there was a fracture of the bone to the nose, together with two linear fractures of the skull. The irregular surface of one end of the instrument thought to have been used was considered responsible for the scattering of small portions of tissue during the attack.

Noline had never given serious thought to religion. She liked to chew gum in public and use colour on her face.

So when Elvis and Joe turned up at her back door late one night 'to talk about the Lord' and then tried to get her naked, she bound them tightly together with duct tape and dialled 911.

Elvis Cookbook

Elvis didn't consider himself to be a drug addict. A drug addict was somebody who stuck a needle in his arm or snorted coke or did all the street drugs. He abhorred those people. Somebody once asked him how he reconciled his drug use with religion and he said, 'Does the Bible tell you not to take Placidyl, and where exactly in the Good Book does it say "Thou shalt not pop a Seconal"?'

One time Elvis got invited to appear on some dumb-ass daytime TV celebrity cooking show. He was scheduled to demonstrate his own special mixture for fudge brownies, which incidentally involved around an ounce of grass, but for the TV show he was going to cut that ingredient out of the recipe.

Anyway, this particular time me and my brother Red, plus a couple of the other guys thought we'd have some fun, so we spike his morning coffee with a 750-milligram tab of acid. Elvis was always pulling stuff like that on us, so we figure that now it's payback time.

So when Veronica, the producer's PA, knocks on his dressing-room door to tell him five minutes to transmission, there's no answer. She knocks again, a little harder this time, but still no answer. There's nothing else for it, so she pushes the door open a crack and peeks in. Elvis is sitting stark naked on the floor in the middle of the room with the toilet seat round his neck. He's eating a box of Kleenex, and he's completely ripped out of his brains. Right after she's stopped screaming, Veronica goes for help. Reinforcements arrive and they finally get Elvis into some clothes and propped up in front of the camera and behind the counter where all the ingredients for the fudge brownies are neatly laid out. Flour, sugar, butter, chocolate and a big tray of eggs.

It's time for the show, so they count Elvis down and away he goes . . .

'Hi, and welcome to today's edition of *Celebrity Cookout*. My name's Elvis Presley and this morning I'd like to show you my very own, very special recipe for fudge brownies, taught to me by Gladys, my mom. I did not bite off the woman's nose. It is not our custom to bite off the nose of a person you have killed. If I kill a man or a woman, someone else bites off the nose. We bite off the noses of people that *others* have killed, we *bite* them off; we do not *cut* them off. I ate a hand of one woman, but it was not the hand of the woman I myself killed. It is not our custom to eat a person we have ourselves killed. But if, after killing a man, you go and sit on a coconut, with also a coconut under each heel, and get your daughter to boil the man's heart, then you may drink the water in which the heart has been boiled. And you may eat a little of the heart also, but you must be sitting on the coconuts all the time. We boil the bodies. We cut them up and boil them in a pot. We boil babies too. We cut them up like a pig. We eat them cold or hot. We eat the legs first. We eat them because they are like fish. We have fudge brownies in the creeks, and cheesy bacon burgers in the trees. But men are our real food.'

There's a short silence, then Elvis's eyes roll back in his head and he slumps face down into the tray of eggs. It was definitely the funniest thing I have ever, ever seen.

About two minutes after that we all get fired.

Twinkletown

Soon as he closed the deal on Twinkletown Farm Elvis changed the name to Circle G. Me an' the guys were real happy about that coz to my way of thinking, 'Let's head back to the Circle G – the G's for Grace-land, baby' sounds a damn sight more manly than 'Hey, honey, let's mosey on back to Twinkletown Farm.'

Circle G Ranch, 150 rolling acres just across the Tennessee border outside Wallis, Mississippi. Elvis poured a fortune into that place. He built a barn, put roads in, sunk a gasoline tank and added extra bedrooms and an office to the house. Then he bought mobile homes for everyone and trucks for all us guys to ride around in.

He'd get out there every day and exercise his horses – play cowboy, wear all that Western crap, the chaps, the hat, the boots, the rancher coat. The happiest we ever saw Elvis was when he first bought that ranch. He looked great, he was off the pills, he had a tan, he even let his hair go back to its natural colour for a while. He caught me out one day, I just couldn't get over how good he looked and I just stood there and stared at him. Finally he broke into a smile and said, 'Shall we dance?'

At night he'd sit in his office and write notes to himself, long lists in thick green marking pen: WHAT I AM GOING TO BUY TOMMORROW, AN ALPHABET FOR MY LORD JESUS, PEOPLE WHO I LIKE. One list read WHY I AM SO HAPPY. Elvis tacked it to the wall right over his desk.

Frankly, it had gotten to be real boring. Me and the guys sat around in our trailers all day talking shit and drinking then at nights we'd go over to the house for supper which Elvis served up for us in the big Western-style kitchen. Simple country fare, beans, chitlins, cornbread, all that kinda homespun flavourless shit. It was like *Little House on the Prairie* and the fucking *Waltons* all rolled into one. Elvis made us say Grace, he talked about Jesus's sweet love and sang gospel songs.

Worst of all he made us wash up all the damn pots. Elvis wrote out a roster in the same green marking pen and tacked it to the wall over the sink. One guy on washing, one on wiping up. He made 'em sing while they worked like they were blacks on a fucking chain-gang. He'd check the stuff over and if he found one godamn speck of food he'd give us all the Cleanliness is next to Godliness shit, make whoever's turn it was do the whole damn lot again and put them back on the roster for the following night.

Anyway, this one particular night we're all sat round the big redwood kitchen table after supper, drinking coffee coz Elvis won't allow booze in the house no more on account of it being the Devil's work. Two of the guys are at the sink. Marty on washing, Lamar on wiping up. Elvis has got 'em singing 'Rawhide'. He's banging an old tin cup on the table to set the tempo and we're all clapping along like some dumb Sunday Bible class.

Now, Marty's been on duty for the last three weeks coz he always fucks up: leaves a fork in the sink, doesn't rinse a plate, forgets a pan or something, and we can see from the poor guy's face that he's really pissed off. Marty finishes up and, as Lamar dries the last pot, Elvis starts the inspection.

Piece by piece he lifts the stuff off the drainer, holds it up to the light to check for crap, then places it on the counter top next to the stove.

'Yeah, fine, fine, good work so far, fellas,' he says, and we're all thinking, great! Way to go, Marty!, an' rooting for the guy like he was in a damn football game when Elvis's face freezes over.

'What in Sweet Jesus's name do you call this?' he says calmly, holding up a dish and stabbing his finger at crumb of something that's so small you'd need a goddamn microscope to take a proper look at it, then shoves all the stuff back into the sink and orders the guys to start over.

So now we're listening to Marty and Lamar singing 'My Way' and filling in with handclaps while they have another try. My kid brother Red stops clapping for a moment and passes me a note under the table which says WE GOTTA GET OUTA HERE.

We finish the song then make an excuse, feed Elvis some dumb shit about a prayer meeting, jump in my truck and head off into Wallis. We hit the nearest bar and after a few beers and a fair amount of bourbon we come up with a plan. Not the greatest plan in the world but a fucking plan all the same. Red drops a quarter in the payphone and calls up the Circle G.

Elvis answers and Red tells him all about the prayer meeting we've just been at and how the preachers been sayin' that Elvis is a fat, talentless, white trash, shit-ass, sex-maniac with greasy hair, dirty songs and no future.

Later, we're driving down the little single-track that leads back to the Circle G, laughing as we imagine Elvis going apeshit coz the fucker never could handle any kinda criticism, and we see headlights coming up towards us real fast. We pull over into the dirt since we figure whoever's driving that other truck ain't gonna be stopping, but it slows down and comes to a halt right alongside us. The window rolls down and we see that it's Marty.

'Hey guys,' he grins. 'Enjoy the prayer meeting?'

Then he tells us Elvis has just gotten some real bad news and he's been sent out for supplies. Now when Elvis uses the word *supplies* that generally means Demerol – the one thing that keeps Elvis from turning into the bug-eyed monster – so we ask Marty where the fuck he's going to get that at this time of night and without a script an all? He laughs and tells us you don't need no script or nothin' for the kind of supplies he's gonna fix up for Elvis this time.

So Marty heads off into Wallis and drops by the Southland mall. They have a Sears down there and it's an all-nighter.

Meanwhile, back at the ranch Elvis is sat bolt upright at the head of the table, eyes bugging out his head and sweat pouring down his face.

An hour later we hear the roar of a Chrysler straight six and see twin headlights cutting across the pasture.

Marty's back.

Marty strolls into the kitchen and plonks three big brown paper sacks down on the table.

'Got the stuff, boss, er, sorry, the supplies,' he grins and he starts unpacking the bags and laying all the shit out in front of Elvis.

'Alrighty, in here we got a hammer, nails and hinges

117

so you can set to fixing up them pasture gates, in here we got eggs, ham, cornbread, flour, coffee, sugar, just the kinda simple honest God-fearing kinda crap you like to eat, an' in here, well, we got you something real, real special.'

Elvis doesn't move, he's staring straight ahead and breathing hard.

Marty pulls a lace-trimmed blue and white gingham apron out of the last bag.

'This is for you, boss, for when you wash up them godamn dishes, real purty ain't it?' and he waves it in front of Elvis's face like a big pansy faggot flag.

Still nothing from the boss, then Marty says, 'Gee, Elvis, you're hurting my feelings now, man, I got this for you coz Jesus told me. Now the least you could do for little Marty is try the motherfucker on you dumb greasy lunk.'

Still no response from Elvis, so Marty drops the loop at the top of the apron over Elvis's head then folds him forward in his chair, ties up the apron strings in a nice neat bow behind his back and pushes Elvis upright in the chair again.

So now Elvis is sat there wearing his brand new pinny and he's still not talking. He sorta looked OK in it – in a kinda fag way. Elvis was a handsome son-ofabitch and he looked good in almost anything.

So I chime in, 'Hey now, Elvis, that is what I call

cool, don't you think so, guys?' and the rest of the guys join in, 'Gee, boss, you're looking good, good, good, looking very fucking good.'

While we're doing this Marty clears up the coffee cups and piles them in front of Elvis, walks over to the sink, pulls the goddamn roster off the wall, wads it up into a ball and tosses it at Elvis. Then he shoves in the plug, the suds, and turns on the faucet.

'Hey Elvis,' he says. 'Your turn now, boss, an' you'd better do it right or little Marty's gonna make you start over, an' over, an' over. Move your ass to that godamn sink.'

'To the sink, to the sink,' we all join in again. 'To the sink, sink, sink, to the motherfucking sink.'

Elvis rises up. Not like he's standing but as if he's being winched up from a hook in the ceiling.

'*Supplies, supplies*,' he says desperately.

'Yeah, sure thing, boss,' says Red. 'No kidding. It is a fucking surprise, an' I never took you for a godamn Chinaman either, man.'

It's not the first time any of us have heard that gag but you had to be there, what else can I tell ya, and while we're all laughing fit to shit we see Elvis walking into the office like he was in zero gravity wearing diving boots or playing Herman Munster in an underwater picture or something and as the laughter dies down we hear this dull clunk and a scream that's kinda not a scream – more like a yelp or a shout cut really short – then another clunk, then the same.

Elvis comes pussy-walking out the office. He flops back down in his chair. The blue and white apron's turning red and now his eyes are clamped tight shut. I take a proper look at Elvis's face, catch a glint of metal through the blood, and figure out what he's done. The crazy fuck's stapled his eyelids together to keep from doing the washing up.

'Looks like we're back to normal,' I say to Marty.

That's the last time I ever laid eyes on the poor little guy.

Loma Linda

I'd arranged to meet Elvis at the railway station after school. It would be our second date. I watched his train pull up to the platform. Elvis jumped off quickly. He ran most of the way home; he would be safer there. When he arrived, his father Vernon was already in, and in the back kitchen the table was set for the evening meal.

'Had a hard day, son? You look worn out.'

'Poison!' Elvis screamed. 'They'll poison you!'

Elvis was admitted to psychiatric hospital the next day. Five days before, he had fallen from a ladder while attempting a paint effect, which he'd seen demonstrated on daytime TV, in one of the guest rooms at Graceland. He had suffered an injury to his head, and remained deeply unconscious for forty-eight hours.

He was sent to an asylum in Loma Linda in the hopes that a change of surroundings, combined with electro-convulsive therapy, would effect some kind of improvement. He was the most outstanding patient in his ward. He wore elaborate, highly coloured clothes, and made it his business to introduce himself to every new nurse as soon as they arrived.

He sincerely believed that he was a major rockstar. He wore a white high-collared jumpsuit covered with rhinestones and brass rings, a wide studded belt which had an enormous American Eagle buckle, a white purple-fringed cape with a prehistoric bird embroidered on the back by his aged alchoholic mother, and amber-tinted aviator shades. Round his neck were several strings of imitation pearls which he refused to take off, even at bathtime. His hair was long, and during the day was held in an untidy bun by numerous hair clips. On his head he wore a tiara made of plastic and decorated with imitation diamonds. He had bought this in Woolworth's for 75 cents on an outing to the seaside in 1967. The effect was completed by brilliant red lipstick, applied so liberally that it made his lips appear twice their normal size.

He refused to eat anything except potatoes. 'These are buried in the ground,' he said, 'and could not be poisoned by radiation.'

Unlike most patients with grandiose delusions, he had the ability to make people feel that they truly were inferior. He used a superior tone with everyone and no one dared laugh at him. The merest hint of a smile, or a word which indicated disrespect, would trigger a stream of abuse. His language would be so obscene that it never failed to produce results. When admonished for his language, which was many times, he would say, 'We rockstars do as we goddamn well please. You are just a fuckin' lackey, an' you better remember that.'

He did very little work on the ward. He considered most of the tasks beneath him, although occasionally he surprised everyone by setting the tables for the midday or evening meal. He refused to take part in industrial therapy, and would never go to the hospital socials or dances. In the evenings he would shut himself into a side room and sort through his belongings, which consisted of old newspapers, cigarette packets and toilet rolls. His collection was jealously guarded, and no one could so much as touch anything without being met with abuse. He was totally involved in his private world, and any attempt to confront him with reality would arouse anger and hostility.

On prom night Elvis came by for me. He'd broken out the nut-house and stolen a car – a blue sedan.

I heard the whine of a siren, Elvis heard it too. 'Jeepers,' he yelled, 'cops,' and before you could say 'Jack Robinson' we were ensconced most comfortably in the sedan and with a cheery squeal of the tyres and a merry blast from the exhaust removal system we roared off down the road at a cracking pace.

'Toodle-pip, you rotten Peelers,' chortled Elvis.

I watched the speedometer climb – forty, fifty, sixty miles an hour and my breath caught in my throat. We left the cop car in the dust. As Elvis slowed up, I let my breath out and leaned back. 'Some crate eh, honey,' said Elvis proudly as we pulled up at a signal.

Then another patrol car pulled up next to us and we were off again, roaring up and down the streets of a residential district. The wind fanned our faces, and the speed filled me with a wild excitement. The police car got ahead of us, but we took a corner on two wheels and passed it. Now, I thought, Elvis will slow up. But he didn't.

'Follow the leader, you silly lady fuckers,' he grinned, glancing casually into the rearviewing mirror arrangement. He flipped the wheel and we swerved off the road on to a lawn around a tree, heading straight for a house.

'Look out – oh look out!' I screamed.

Elvis swung the wheel and we were out on the road again. He was laughing. 'What's the matter, chicken? Didn't you like the new driveway I gave that place?'

Just then Barbara Cartland tottered out into the road, the sedan's tyres squealed angrily as Elvis snatched at the wheel to stop us from wasting the crazy old bird. My mouth was dry, but the rest of me was wringing wet. Elvis reached over and squeezed my knee and it was like an electric shock running through my body. He loved me, he really did! Me, Angie Crumbaker and, boy, was I glad now that I was missing the prom.

As we roared on down the road, I had a feeling I'd never felt before. It's hard to describe, but I felt like I never wanted to be anywhere but there. The faster we went, the more the blood seemed to race through my veins. My cheeks tingled, and I was alive all over. It was like being on a rollercoaster ride – so scary and yet so thrilling.

Again I heard the whine of another siren. Again Elvis heard it too. 'Jeepers,' he yelled again. 'Cops again!'

Elvis wheeled the sedan around a corner, up the street and out on to the highway. Seventy, eighty, ninety – we were almost flying!

Barbara Cartland staggered out in front of us again, and this time we got the bitch exactly square-on. I felt a sickening, thrilling jolt of malevolent teenage delight as her misshapen, shrivelled old body bounced off the windshield straight into the path of a monster truck which had sharpened electrified spikes protruding from every one of its fourteen greasy axles.

Elvis flicked on the wipers to clear away some of the

blood, shit and strips of fossilised orange flesh. In the rearview mirror I could see the flashing blue light of the police car light growing bigger and bigger.

We darted in and out of the traffic. Then, just before we got to a bridge, Elvis swung the sedan off the highway and down a little dirt road. As we bumped over the potholes he slowed down and we came to a standstill in a dry river bed under the bridge. It was dark under there and my heart was pounding so hard I was afraid that Elvis would hear it.

The siren wailed closer and closer. It was right over our heads! Then it faded as the cops sped past us, over the bridge and away down the highway.

'Have a good trip, Motherfucker,' Elvis yelled, leaning out the window and waving.

'Turn on the radio,' he said, 'so we can keep track of the time,' then at last he fell silent.

I sat there in the darkness, listening to the soft wild throb of the music, and I trembled. I felt his arm slide around my shoulders, then his hand was on my cheek, turning my face to his. Shivers ran through me, and my heart pounded in my throat. Suddenly Elvis was kissing me long and hard. I couldn't breathe. I felt so very happy. I thought I'd suffocate. I managed to turn my face away from his for a moment and then I felt his hands tighten around my throat.

Yorkshire Elvis

I decided to go fully tooled-up for this little trip, just in case.

I carried a .38 snub-nosed detective special because it had solid killing power, a large capacity clip, and was accurate at a distance. I also carried a .25 calibre, semi-automatic handgun. And I had a razor-sharp, double-edged buck knife in one boot. I also had a .38 short-barrel revolver, a powerful weapon ideal for close combat. I knew to shoot in the stomach to cause the victim's hand to relax instantly, preventing my getting shot by a bullet fired by reflex at death. And I was skilled enough to shoot the person in the head, an instant kill, with no danger of a reflex action at the moment of death.

I'm not telling you this to show off. Personally, I love violence, can't get enough of it, but on this occasion I intended to use my special skills only if I had to. I meant to get away alive and unhurt. But I would take a life in an instant if those bastards got nasty.

Just to be on the safe side, I carried some specialist

equipment with me, grappling hooks on ropes, thin nylon cord, a flash light, first-aid kit, snakebite kit, emergency tent, water purification pills, an axe, insect-repellent nets, hand grenades and dynamite, a cross-bow, gags, duct tape and distress flares.

I crept out of the house and stole noiselessly up the hill, trying not to draw attention to myself. I got to the place and eased open the door. I was tense now, hyped-up but not scared. I edged towards the counter and slipped a £10 note under the armoured-glass partition. I could feel my heart pounding and hear the blood rushing in my ears, but I was OK – still in complete control.

'Two electricity tokens please, love,' I said without a trace of fear.

Yorkshire Elvis: Part Two

I wait while the wife goes out. Then I go upstairs and fold back a corner of the front bedroom net. I peer through the window to check. I make sure the coast is clear. I watch as the hood of her duffel coat disappears round the corner by the so-called temporary bus stop they put there last February after the real one got burned down. I wait till I hear the rumble of a big diesel and the hiss of air-assisted brakes so I know she's on it and not forgotten anything. I know she's not coming back. She's not going to catch me. She'll be gone for at least two hours. Me, I go downstairs, put the chain on the front door and drop the latch on the Yale so's I won't be disturbed. Then I go back upstairs again.

I enter the spare bedroom, lie down on the fluffy brown carpet, stretch out my arms and drag the equipment from under the bed. I kick off my slippers, roll over on to my belly and feel the soft pile tickling up between my toes. First off, and just to get me in the mood, I like to flick through a few magazines. There's a lovely American model in one of them that I'm keen on at the moment, and the pictures, especially the detail you get in the close-ups, helps me with ideas of my own. I ease back the zip on the big canvas bag, unpack my equipment and lay it all out on the bed. Next I go into the bathroom and lock the door. I carefully unsnap the injection-moulded avocado bath panel and prop it up against the basin. Then I find the loose floorboard, slide it out, and reach down between the joists.

I take out the box, lift the lid, peel back a thick layer of cotton wool and for the first time in a week I see her. For a while I just kneel and gaze down at her. Slowly, I stretch out my hand to stroke her. A loud knocking at the front door stops me short. My hand hovers over the box.

Somebody's thumping so hard it sounds like they'll put it through. On this estate that kind of knock can only be the club-book man or the police, only it can't be the club-book as we don't owe this month. I go downstairs and peer through the spy-hole. It is the police, two of them, a lad who only looks about fourteen and an older WPC. They knock again. My head's pressed hard up against the door, so this time the sound goes right through me.

There's nothing for it so I take the chain off. My heart's pounding as I unlatch the Yale and open the front door. They smile and introduce themselves.

There's a little girl gone missing and they need to ask me a few questions, just routine and it'll only take five minutes. They show me her photo. She's wearing school uniform and holding a certificate; she looks very serious. I stand barefoot in the doorway answering their questions. I tell them I've never seen her before, the blood rushing in my ears, all the while thinking about the box, the picture in the magazine, and my equipment laid out on the bed.

They thank me and leave. I watch them go down our path, out the gate, up next door's path, and I hear them knock again. I fasten our front door and run back upstairs.

I lock myself in the bathroom. I kneel on the floor by the box. I feel uneasy, panicky, and my stomach twists up. I need to get wood. I know I've got a problem.

Then I have an idea, so I unlock the bathroom door, go out on to the landing and open the airing-cupboard door. The old ironing board's propped up in there, the one the wife's mother gave us after we got married. The wife doesn't need it any more, she's got a new metal one with a flowery padded cover permanently set up in the kitchen. My hands are shaking as I lift out the old board and peel back six inches of the frayed stripy material it's covered with. Underneath there's just what I need to see and I become very excited. I carry the ironing board through to the spare bedroom, pull off the rest of the fabric, and lie down on the floor. I settle into the soft carpet and unroll my drawings. When I've worked out exactly what I'm going to do next, I go back into the bathroom for the box. Cradling it in my arms I take it into the spare room and set it on the bed. I lift her out and run my hands over her body. I feel very happy now and much calmer. I reach for the Vaseline and my syringe.

At the moment I'm working on a 1/32 scale version of Jenny. When I first saw her stretched across the centre pages of my favourite magazine, she took my breath away, and I knew that she was the one for me. She's a two-seat trainer, a biplane, Model N° JN4 – nicknamed 'Jenny' by the young American pilots she helped learn to fly; wing-span forty-four feet, length twenty-seven feet, originally manufactured in 1914 by the Curtiss Aeroplane and Motors Corporation and powered by a single 90hp Curtiss OX-5 engine.

I've pretty much done the fuselage, a thin wooden frame covered with fabric and aluminium sheeting – Baco Foil in this case – around the engine bay and exhaust pipes. So far it's taken me three months to dot the rivets on using my own secret technique. Hours of painstaking work, minute quantities of Marvin Medium squeezed from a syringe. I found the syringe in the shelter before it burned down, soaked it in bleach for forty-eight hours to kill anything nasty, and now I use it to apply the glue and to introduce tiny amounts of silver paint to create a metallic effect. Looking at the fuselage now, it's so perfect that I come over a bit funny. It doesn't seem possible that it's all my own work and I am so proud.

The old ironing board is solid spruce. Beautiful straight-grained planks, perfectly seasoned, bone-dry from years in the warm cupboard, and there's loads of it. Just what I need to make the wings. I rub Vaseline on to the gleaming blue carbon-steel blade of my freshly sharpened tenon saw and begin the first cut.

I've always made models, ever since I was a kid. Two years after we married the wife banned them from the house, said she didn't want the mess, the noise, the smell of paint and me turning the kitchen into a workshop every evening. Anyway, she said it was queer, a grown man messing about with toy aeroplanes.

So I wait while the wife goes out.

My Elvis Blackout

I took a final drag from my cigarette, hanging on to it like it was a last request, and then dropped the butt into the toilet before changing bravely into my crappy costume, then I slicked back my hair and glued on my furry sideburns.

The booing and cheering in the hall had become more spiteful, and I heard my backing tape start up.

I walked out past the Durex machine and on to the tiny stage. The crowd looked ugly and very pissed, some people were flicking beermats and gobbing even before I started to sing.

I took a deep breath and launched into my first number, 'Look at What Happened to My Leg' . . . A beermat bounced off my forehead, and then three of the women nearest the stage grabbed the microphone lead and yanked it with all their might. The jack plug pinged out of the amplifier and the speakers were silent. At that moment it came to me that I was undoubtedly the worst club singer in the whole world.

It seemed ironic that a pathetic lightbulb hardly

strong enough to light my face as I stood beneath it could now so cruelly expose a bald spot shining through black, silver-rooted hair as I bent over to fiddle with the jack plug.

My belly hung over the wide-buckled and much-studded belt while I endeavoured to re-plug the microphone. Giving up at last I stood there smiling as abuse and missiles rained down upon me, I nodded with appreciation like an opera singer being showered with flowers.

Right now the only thing I had in common with an opera singer was that I was a fat bastard.

From Elvis's Secret Diary:
Part Three

I'm ten. At junior school, Miss Levin is our teacher for everything. In maths, she shows us a sheet of squared graph paper.

'This is a million,' she says.

So now, whenever I think of a million, that is what I see. Later, when she tells us that the Nazis murdered six million Jews, I visualise sheets filled with tiny squares and just how many corpses that must have been.

I try to think of each square filled up with a miniature passport photograph, and how long it would take if I could just sit and listen to each of those people say their name. I decide that it can't be true.

*

Fifteen. I'm watching *The World at War* on Sunday afternoon. I should be revising for my O level mocks. A bulldozer is pushing a pile of emaciated bodies into a pit. They slither down its sides and come to rest, arms and legs and heads entwined together and sticking out of the heap at unnatural angles. Now the camera pans across a long room; there are pails filled with gold teeth, mountains of rags, a heap of artificial limbs, and a tangle of spectacle frames, meshed together like a giant wire hairnet.

Monday morning I'm sat in my mock, trying to think of the French words for 'silver birch'. I close my eyes and see a million tiny squares filled with spectacles.

From Elvis's Secret Diary:
Part Four

I'm five. I'm playing out in the drive on my bike, a Raleigh Tomahawk with stabilisers. I get bored with that, and take a trowel from the greenhouse. I go up the road and squeeze between a dead tree and a clapboard fence. I'm hollowing the tree out from the back so that I can live there when I'm older. I squat in the base of the tree and chop at its powdery insides with the point of the trowel. Then I feel poorly and go back home.

Later, I'm in the car in Leicester. Mom opens the car door and holds me out, my head over the gutter, I'm sick, it's a greeny-orange colour, people are staring.

It's two weeks later, I'm in an isolation ward in Leicester Royal Infirmary. I was thin before but now I'm really skinny, and my hands look like paper. A nurse comes in. She's got a big dish of Rice Crispies with too much milk, much more than I can have at home. 'Try and eat these,' she says, then my mom comes in, she says I've been asleep for two weeks. She's got a new brooch on, it looks like knights sitting round a hubcap.

I'm fifteen. My teeth are sticking out all over the place. I have a double row at the bottom and so five good teeth are taken out. I wake up the next day with a big lump of red jelly in my gob.

I have a brace top and bottom, I look like the bad guy in the Bond films, only skinnier. There's so much saliva sloshing around I have to take the braces out and rinse them at break-time. I've got the best French accent in my class.

Once a week I go to Mr Robinson on Granby Street to have them adjusted. 'How are we today?' he asks. 'Farn thunks,' I say, biting his fingers. Then he comes at me with a giant pair of pliers, right up to my mouth. He whips the braces out and tightens them with the pliers. He does this every week and thinks it's highly amusing.

I put the braces back in. They feel so tight it's like my head's going to implode. 'See you next week,' he says. 'Ukey,' I say, hardly able to move my jaws.

This goes on for eighteen months and one day he tells my mom, 'Thats it! By the way, the X-rays show his wisdom teeth are impacted. They'll have to come out when he's older – that's a hospital job, I'm afraid.'

I feel like there's a bomb in my mouth.

Elvis Spotter's Guide

A tall glass display case containing three human skeletons, all of them former Elvis impersonators. On each skeleton, the fifth cervical vertebra, picked out by a red ribbon, has been crushed. Beneath each skeleton is the high collar of the prisoner's stage shirt, roughly cut off with scissors. This is done a few moments before the execution to ensure that the true fall of the blade is not impeded. Two guards hold him, and a third approaches him with the shears and starts cutting.

The prisoner feels the cold steel against his neck as it cuts through his shirt.

He paled slightly at the sight of the scaffold, but recovered by the time he got to the top of the steps. He tried to address the people, but was given no time; his fichu was torn off his neck and, in a moment, his head rolled to the ground. One of the executioner's assistants, a follower of Marat called Legros, ran his knife up the severed neck and held the head high to show it to the crowd. He gave it two or three hard slaps, and the face was seen to blush – not only the cheek that was slapped, but both cheeks, exactly as if he were still able to feel emotion. The spectators were appalled, and a tremor of horror ran through the murmuring crowd.

The body lies outstretched on a board, supported by two trestles. The head is placed near the trunk; the arms hang down to the ground; the cadaver is still dressed in a white robe, the upper part of which is bloody. One person, holding a torch in one hand and an instrument (some kind of speculum) in the other, seems to be stripping Elvis of his clothing. Four others are bending forwards, examining the body attentively.

At the head we find two individuals, one of whom wears the tricolour belt; the other extends his hands as if to say, 'Here is the body, look.'

Acknowledgments

A selection of these stories appeared in a Clocktower Press booklet in 1998. Others have been published in *Deliberately Thirsty* and *Nerve* magazine. Thanks to Lorraine Butler, Duncan McLean, Sean Bradley, Adam Sutherland, Todd McEwen, Andy Eccleston, Steve Scott, Catriona Finlayson, Victoria Hobbs and all at Ye Olde Shakespeare Inn for their encouragement and support.

A Note on the Author

Born in Leicestershire, Simon Crump studied
philosophy at Sheffield University and has
lived in Sheffield for the last twenty years. An
internationally exhibited artist, he has lectured
in fine art and photography at various universities
and more recently worked as a curatorial assistant
in a medical museum. His stories have appeared in
numerous magazines and anthologies. He is the author
of the forthcoming *Monkey's Birthday & Other
Stories*, published by Bloomsbury in Spring 2002.

A Note on the Type

The text of this book is set in Linotype Sabon, named after the type founder, Jacques Sabon. It was designed by Jan Tschichold and jointly developed by Linotype, Monotype and Stempel, in response to a need for a typeface to be available in identical form for mechanical hot metal composition and hand composition using foundry type.

Tschichold based his design for Sabon roman on a fount engraved by Garamond, and Sabon italic on a fount by Granjon. It was first used in 1966 and has proved an enduring modern classic.